11

ANTHONY MASTERS

HAUNTINGS

NOBODY'S CHILD

When he looked back he was sure that the arm had moved another few centimetres towards him. The minute hand was stretched out in his direction. Jess felt vomit rising in his throat and he hurled himself bodily at the door. It didn't move at all and he backed away, accidentally treading on the hand. When he looked down he saw that he had broken it into four pieces and that each piece was moving towards him like a scurrying insect.

Other titles in the HAUNTINGS series:

Ghost Abbey by Robert Westall
Don't Go Near the Water by Carolyn Sloan
Voices by Joan Aiken
The Nightmare Man by Tessa Krailing
A Wish at the Baby's Grave by Angela Bull
The Bone Dog by Susan Price
All on a Winter's Day by Lisa Taylor
Old Man on a Horse by Robert Westall
The Rain Ghost by Garry Kilworth
The Haunting of Sophie Bartholomew by
Elizabeth Lindsay

11

ANTHONY MASTERS

HAUNTINGS

NOBODY'S CHILD

Hippo Books
Scholastic Publications Limited
London

Scholastic Publications Ltd.,
10 Earlham Street, London WC2H 9RX, UK

Scholastic Inc.,
730 Broadway, New York, NY 10003, USA

Scholastic Tab Publications Ltd.,
123 Newkirk Road, Richmond Hill,
Ontario L4C 3G5, Canada

Ashton Scholastic Pty. Ltd.,
P O Box 579, Gosford, New South Wales,
Australia

Ashton Scholastic Ltd.,
165 Marua Road, Panmure, Auckland 6,
New Zealand

First published by Scholastic Publications Limited, 1989

ISBN 0 590 76119 6

Made and printed by Cox & Wyman Ltd, Reading, Berks
Typeset in Plantin by AKM Associates (UK) Ltd., Southall, London

To Richard Hoyes, Kim Gayner and their students who helped to bring this book alive.

Chapter One

He had heard the noise – a metallic rattling – when he was only a few steps down the spiral staircase. Curious, Jess had come racing back and found it there. There was no slope; the roller skate had crossed about six metres of dormitory floor of its own volition.

The sound of laughing and swearing floated up to him from the courtyard. An old caravan served as a rest room for the demolition gang to brew tea and eat their sandwiches. The walls were covered with lurid pin-ups. It was the last place that Jess wanted to be – mainly because of the teasing.

He knelt down by the roller skate and stared at it. It hadn't even been standing the right way up. There were dozens of them rusting on their sides in a pile on the floor. How could it have come free and got itself upright, let alone run unaided across the cracked lino of the floor? Suddenly he stiffened. Could it have been a joke? There had been so many of them recently and all aimed at him. They probably thought he was daft, mooning round these deserted rooms, and it would please them to have fun with him. But how had they done it? He looked for a string or some other evidence of a trick – but there was none.

Jess crossed the dormitory and went to look outside the door and into the bathroom. But there was only the spider-ridden porcelain bath and the plaster dust that liberally covered the floor. He was alone. He had to be. Back in the dormitory he sat on a broken-down chair and stared at the roller skate. It was utterly still. If he didn't touch it, the skate would remain still for ever. Jess picked it up and nursed it in his hands. The metal was cold and the rust was everywhere. Outside a whistle shrilled and he got up reluctantly and returned the roller skate to the pile. Then he turned on his heel and clattered down the circular staircase.

The teasing had started directly Jess had taken on the holiday job with the demolition gang. They had no time for an inarticulate fourteen-year-old, and only wanted a tea boy and someone to clear the rubbish out of the rooms of the old orphanage. A great turreted and porticoed pile, Holloway House stood in its own grounds by the railway track. Built in the late nineteenth century, the words "Holloway House Orphanage" were carved into the stonework facing the railway line. Jess had passed the place every day of his life and had hardly given the building a second thought until he saw the demolition boards. The house had been empty for a few years; fostering had made Holloway House redundant.

Jess had known one of the last orphans to live at Holloway House when he was at Middle School.

Tom had not been a close friend, but he had once invited Jess to a Christmas party there. It had been quite special. In the great hall there was a very small Christmas tree. Portraits of past matrons stared severely down from the walls and the six remaining children sat round a table drawn up to a big open fireplace in which a log fire roared and crackled. The rest of the hall was completely bare of furniture. Matron sat at the head of the table and, at first, she had looked as severe as the surrounding portraits. But when tea was over – and it was a particularly good tea – Miss Paxton had become a different person. They played all kinds of games and Miss Paxton had joined in them all herself, shouting with joy and running around so fast that her hair slipped away from its bun and flowed down her neck making her look, for a moment, like a young girl. Jess was shy and inhibited but he had joined in – which was more than he was prepared to do in the giggly atmosphere of the school disco. It had been a very memorable evening indeed, which he had treasured long after he had forgotten Tom.

The mystery of the moving roller skate faded from Jess's mind when he met Wayne at the bottom of the stairs. Of all his tormentors Wayne was the worst. Small, dark and Italian looking, with a ready wit and a sharp tongue, Wayne had been the first to notice Jess's concern for the old toys and artefacts that still littered the floors of the orphanage, carelessly left to the mercy of the demolition company. He had been delighted when he had first discovered Jess taking home a very old and battered elephant. "Gonna give him a kiss and cuddle then?" was the predictable comment that he repeated hour after hour, with his mates taking up the mockery in gleeful chorus.

"Been stocking up your toy cupboard then?" Wayne laughed as he pushed past him and Jess gave him a sickly grin. If it wasn't for the money he'd chuck in the first real holiday job he had ever taken on. But he and Mum needed the money so much. Ever since Dad's sudden death they had been well below the poverty line and Jess was determined to get any job that would bring in a bit more money for them both. However strong his budding hatred of Wayne, he had made up his mind that he was going to stick to it – somehow.

It was drizzling when he emerged from the front entrance of the house. The light summer rain that had been falling all day gave an even more melancholy appearance to the garden that was already covered in rubble and tyre marks. Jess walked towards the foreman's caravan, longing for the end of the summer holidays and his final pay day. Ever since he had started, he had had the mickey taken out of him and although some of the teasing was gentle some of it was not. Jess had neither the confidence nor the resources to answer back, for although he was tall and physically strong he was also shy and insecure. He had been adopted when he was a baby and the death of his father had shattered him. The short but intense illness and the inability of the doctor to cure him had at first made Jess incredulous and then isolated. He had not seen much of his friends ever since, had not practised with the league football team, already in training for the autumn fixtures, and had stayed at home with Mum as much as he could. She needed his support anyway, he thought, as they went for their regular Saturday walk in the park or sat at home watching the telly. Mum had been as shattered as he was so they needed to support each other, Jess told himself when he refused a trip to the cinema or to the swimming pool with his friends yet again.

"You're looking a bit down, aren't you, young fellow?" Bill Langridge was the foreman on the site and the only person that Jess really liked. He was roughly kind and, like Jess, detached from the others. He sat on his own in the site office a good deal, a cup of tea in front of him, staring at the plans of the old building, and working out how to demolish each section safely, beginning with the outbuildings. But Jess often thought Bill's mind was on something else as he sat there, and wondered what it was. He was a big untidy sort of man with a balding head. The only neat thing about him was his little brown moustache which the others called his Hitler tash.

"I'm O.K."

"They been getting at you?"

Jess looked at him, startled. He had assumed that his persecution had gone unnoticed.

"You're doing well here, lad."

"Thanks."

"You're strong and willing but you got feelings."

Jess said nothing.

"Sit down a minute."

Jess sat down dutifully on the little canvas chair alongside the old stained table that served as Mr Langridge's desk.

"Why don't you call me Bill?"

"O.K." Jess was wary. He didn't like surprises of any kind now – not after Dad's death.

"Don't let them get you down."

"They're all right." Jess shrugged miserably.

"They're not." Bill was indignant. "Most of those blokes are no-hopers. A few of the older ones are O.K.

but most of them young 'uns – thick as planks and going nowhere. Casual labour, that's all they are. *They* got no feelings. Now you – you got feelings like."

"Too many, probably." Jess laughed uncomfortably.

"Maybe. But, for instance, you feel something about this old place, don't you?"

"What do you mean?" Jess was immediately suspicious.

"Them old toys and stuff. You been taking them home."

"You said no one would want them," he replied defensively.

"And I meant it. But you *care* for them, don't you?"

Jess shrugged. "I just don't like to see them chucked away."

"You feel something else though, don't you?" Bill was insistent.

"I don't know what you mean."

"Yes, you do. Don't be frightened, son. My wife and I are mediums. We pick up this kind of thing."

So that was the extra dimension, thought Jess. He stared at Bill, not able to make up his mind whether he was a crank or not.

"I know what you're thinking." Bill grinned.

"What?" Jess was worried. Could he read minds as well?

"You're thinking I'm a right old crank, aren't you?"

"No." Jess lied.

"Yes you are. Come on, old son. Don't be so afraid of me."

"Well – I don't know anything about mediums, do I?"

"No, you probably don't, and I don't intend to start telling you or like as not I'll have your mum after me. But I will tell you this: places which had a lot of living in them leave behind a kind of vibration. This place. It's had kids in it for years. Decades. Laughing and crying and living. They must have left their mark here. They must have left a vibration. Mustn't they?"

Jess remembered the inexplicable moving of the roller skate. It had happened only half an hour ago. "They might," he said cautiously.

"I can feel it. You can feel it. Isn't that right?"

"All old places —" Jess began rather feebly.

"And this one in particular. I've knocked down some old buildings in me time but this one – it's still living, isn't it?" He looked down at the schedule on his desk. "By the end of the month this place will be flattened and the vibrations will have gone. Every time I walk down the corridors – in the big hall or in matron's old office or the gym or the dormitories or anywhere else – I can feel it. And I know you can too."

"Would I be a medium then?"

Bill laughed, returning them abruptly to normality. "I don't know about that. But I'll tell you this: us two can feel it but those louts can't. So we got something in common, haven't we?"

"I suppose we have."

"So don't mind the ribbing. Come to me if it gets too bad."

Jess knew that he wouldn't but he nodded his agreement.

"Now I tell you what you can do. You know that glass display case in the front hall?"

"Yes."

"It's full of soldiers and model tanks."

"That's right."

"Why don't you take it down and give it a real good dusting. Then you could take that home too – if you like."

Jess was suddenly touched by the raw kindness of the big rambling man. "I will. Thanks very much."

"By the way –"

"Yes?"

"You know that kid, Wayne?"

"Yes."

"He's the worst of the bunch. Real trouble maker. I'd like an excuse to get rid of him. Let me know if he gets at you."

Jess knew that he wouldn't grass on Wayne, but again he nodded agreement as he got up and left the site office. He was glad they'd had a talk; he needed a friend.

Chapter Two

"What's all this?" asked his mum, when Jess arrived home.

Jess had staggered back to his house on the estate, carrying the display cabinet with the soldiers and models carefully packed in a cardboard box.

"Bill, the foreman at work – he gave it to me."

"More junk?" But she was smiling. His mother was a tall, rather blundering sort of woman who was often clumsy and would sit and cry at her own mistakes. She had done that well before her husband's death and Jess and his dad had loved her for her ineptitude. She was a deeply kind and spiritual person who would often come home with abandoned animals which she would also cry over. Her hobby was music. She had always sung in a local choir, but since Dad had died she had not gone, or indeed listened to any music at all. She said she couldn't bear to, that she would just never stop crying if she did. Jess knew she was making the same mistakes as he was, but somehow neither of them could shake themselves out of their lethargy and their persistent need for each other.

"Are you going to watch the serial?" she asked.

He nodded and looked at his watch. "I'll just nip upstairs and arrange these," he said, and she smiled.

"I've smashed another of those patterned plates. We've only got two left now."

"Doesn't matter, Mum. They were only cheap."

For the first time since Dad had died he felt a flash of irritation and suddenly realized that he needed to get away from her. He just wanted to be alone with the cabinet and the models. Jess hurried up to his room, leaving her staring up the stairs after him. He wondered if she had noticed his impatience. They were so close now that they hardly needed to speak to communicate.

In his room, Jess dumped the cabinet on the floor and began to arrange the soldiers and the model tanks on his table. They were still very dusty, so he found an old toothbrush and very carefully began to clean them. His room was full of things from Holloway House now. There was the old elephant, badly faded and missing a trunk. He planned to repair it as soon as he could. There was an old dolls-house – just the inside and part of the roof – and there were books, largely adventure annuals of the fifties, a deflated football, a doll with no face and an old game of Monopoly with most of the cards missing. Jess knew there would be more to come.

For an hour he worked on, quite oblivious of the time, and he was again irritated when he heard the knock on the door. He called out to his mum and she came in hesitantly, looking both accusing and bewildered.

"You missed the serial."

He half rose. "I'm sorry, Mum. I forgot the time."

"I didn't like to shout up."

"You should've."

"You never miss it."

"I'm sorry, Mum." Again he felt the unfamiliar spurt of annoyance. What did it matter about the serial? Then he said, "Shall I come down?"

"Not if you're busy." There was a wistful note in her voice.

"I'll just finish this then." He turned away.

"Your supper will be ready soon. Shall I shout?"

"Of course." He turned back to his dusting and she went away.

That night, Jess dreamt that the football was inflated and was bouncing around his bedroom. The football bounced higher and higher and Jess watched it coming for him. Then it hit him sharply on the nose and he woke up. His nose felt funny and he rubbed at it and then looked down in the half light. He had forgotten to close the curtains properly, and thin moonlight was straggling through to illuminate a patch of light on the floor. Inside it lay the football – still deflated.

After that he couldn't sleep but lay watching the dolls-house. Some of the rooms were still furnished, although most of the furnishings were broken. The kitchen was the most intact with a tiny ironing board and sink and fridge and cupboards. Then he noticed that one of the cupboard doors was open and inside there was something that he had not noticed before. It was a miniature football – a tiny nut-like object. He looked back at the deflated football, heard a noise and glanced back at the dolls-house cupboard. The tiny football was now on the kitchen floor, and as he watched it it began to bounce. It must have bounced five or six times before Jess jumped out of bed.

Immediately he set foot on the floor it stopped bouncing. He knelt down and stared at the miniature kitchen in amazement, then he reached out and touched the ball. The deadly cold ate into his finger. He withdrew it and then touched the ball again. This time it was a little warmer but not much. Jess continued to stare at it until he fell asleep. He did not see it move again.

Next morning Jess could not disentangle what he had dreamt and what he had actually witnessed. In the end, because it had all merged together, he decided that he must have dreamt everything. At breakfast he was tired and even more irritable than he had been the night before.

"Anything happen at work yesterday?" His mother stood there, defenceless, in her flowered apron. She had already knocked over the orange juice, and as she mopped it up, he could see that she was very nervous. But somehow he hardened his heart.

"No."

"You just seem a bit —" She broke off and stared at him.

"A bit what?" He removed the top of his egg to find it hard boiled and the irritation was replaced by real anger. "It's hard boiled."

"Sorry, dear."

"And the toast's cold."

"Shall I make you some more? Boil you another egg?"

"No."

"What's the matter, love? It's not like you to be

ratty. Is that job getting you down? You don't have to do it. You're looking *so* tired."

"I told you I'm fine." He got up and reached for his bag. "I'm off."

"But you haven't had any breakfast." She practically wrung her hands and he felt the anger boiling inside him and the love fighting back and losing.

"I'll be fine."

"Don't forget your sandwiches."

He gave her a swift peck on the cheek, grabbed his sandwiches and banged his way out.

It was a softly warm late August morning. The summer had been awful but today the sun was shining. Jess walked towards Holloway House, his spirits low and a leaden headachy feeling inside him. He felt really lousy, but it was not that he didn't want to go to work. Suddenly he longed to be in Holloway House again, although he hoped that Bill would put him on more clearing duty and he would not have to go anywhere near the others. He wanted to be up in the dormitory, looking at the roller skates. Jess thought about his dream and saw again the miniature football, bouncing.

The next moment he was falling, deafened and stunned by the screaming brakes. When he focused he found himself lying in the road with the bumper of a car a couple of centimetres away from his head.

"What the hell do you think you're doing?" The motorist, pin-striped and sweating, was shaking with combined fear and fury. "You just walked out in front of me."

Jess looked up at the puffy face and sweating brow. "You idiot," he said. He struggled to his feet, surprised that he was not hurt. He felt the unfamiliar anger rise and rise.

"I beg your pardon?"

"You're stupid, aren't you?"

The man spluttered in righteous indignation. "I'll have you know that if I hadn't slammed on my brakes you'd have been a goner."

A little crowd was gathering, faster now that they could hear shouting.

"You were going too damn fast." Jess was trembling with anger. "You want to watch out."

"I was crawling along. That's what saved you." The motorist looked round but there was no sign of the police. He got back in his car. "You're a mindless little twit," he informed Jess, as he drove off.

Jess aimed a kick at the car and missed. "Out of my way," he yelled, as he pushed through the crowd. They fell back respectfully. He felt an unusual sense of power and no surprise at his out-of-character behaviour. As Jess neared Holloway House, his anger cooled and a curious sense of relief overtook him. He felt calm and relaxed; it was as if he was coming home.

"Jess?"

He sat up amongst the pile of roller skates, pleased and happy to hear the friendly call.

"Yes, Matron?" The words were out of his mouth before he could stop them, but they had seemed natural enough.

Bill stood on the threshold of the dormitory, staring down at him in bewilderment. "What did you call me?"

Jess shook his head. There were unfamiliar sounds inside it and the smell of frying food was in his nostrils. Then the confusion disappeared – and so did the delicious smell. "Bill." He said the name quietly.

"You haven't reported in."

"Sorry."

"You must always report to me in the morning. If you don't, I won't know where you are." He spoke slowly and kindly, as if he was talking to someone he was very fond of.

"I thought I'd make a start up here."

"What are you doing?"

"I was going to clear this floor and get some of the old beds out and burn them." He spoke quickly, almost excitedly.

Bill visibly relaxed. "That's O.K. then. But remember to report to me directly you arrive. I thought you was ill or something."

"Sorry."

"You don't look that good."

"I'm fine. Honest."

"You looked knackered, son."

Bill's persistent questioning did not irritate Jess in the least. He felt calm and relaxed; at home.

"Had a bit of a sleepless night. But I feel fine now."

"Nothing you want to tell me?"

"Nothing."

Bill stared down at him for quite some time. Then he turned and walked away, looking disappointed and somehow let down. Jess knew how delighted Bill would have been if he had told him about last night. But he didn't want to. It was his secret.

Chapter Three

The railway line ran behind Holloway House, at the bottom of the grounds. The back wall of the house was still covered in signs saying "Orphanage" and "Donations Welcome" so that passengers on the passing trains could be reminded of its existence and its need for funds.

There was still a derelict garden, and rusted swings, concrete tubes and a roundabout that creaked round on a rusted mechanism lay in the long, unkempt grass. It was only a wooden circle with a handrail, but Jess, making sure that he was unobserved, would often sit on it and slowly turn.

Jess stoked the bonfire he had made and watched the old wooden bedsteads burn. Then he climbed on to the roundabout and looked at his watch. Half eleven. They knocked off in an hour and he would find a place to have his sandwiches. It was very hot and he had taken off his shirt. Sweating slightly as he pushed the roundabout into clumsy motion he felt a cooling breeze fan his bare skin. He closed his eyes, smelling cocoa and hot milk and toast and baked beans. Someone was singing very softly. It was an old song and the voice was a distant treble. Cool fingers gently touched his chest and then his forehead, but even as he thought he recognized the cool hand it slapped him round the back of the neck.

Jess opened his eyes and saw Wayne laughing in front of him. He was stripped down to just a pair of shorts and he looked lithe and muscular despite his small size.

"Having a little ride then?" his voice cooed, and his dark eyes flashed in Mediterranean jest.

Immediately, the anger returned to Jess like a solid weight. Then, like a spring, it uncoiled. "Get off."

"Eh?"

"Get your filthy hands off me."

"Don't you speak that way to me, little boy."

"I'll speak to you any way I like." He got off the roundabout, planted a hand on Wayne's chest and shoved him away.

Wayne's dark features flushed. "I'll fix you for that." He came at Jess, his fists flailing, but the anger was still mounting in Jess and he was there more quickly. For a few seconds they rained blows on each other and then clinched. Jess could feel Wayne trying to throw him on to the ground, but just then a shout rang out from one of the orphanage windows and they sprang apart, panting.

"Wayne!"

Bill was staring down at them.

"You can collect your cards, Wayne. I told you before to leave that kid alone."

Before Wayne could splutter into speech, Jess intervened. "It was my fault, Mr Langridge."

"What?" Bill looked down at him unbelievingly.

"I said it was my fault - honest."

"Blimey."

"So don't blame him. Please."

Jess went back to the bonfire and began to stoke it, leaving Wayne to stare up at Bill ingratiatingly.

"That's true. He went for me."

"I don't believe it."

"Ask him."

"All right. I'll let you off this time but listen to me, young Wayne —"

"I'm listening."

"You step out of line just one more time and you're for the high jump. Got it?"

"I got it." Wayne slowly walked away and Bill's head disappeared from the window.

Left on his own, Jess began to whistle the melody that he had heard sung while he was on the roundabout. At first he did not recognize it. Then he realized he was whistling "*Home Sweet Home*".

Jess had lunch on his own in the garden and then spent the afternoon collecting more old furniture and dragging it down the stairs to burn. It was good physical work and despite the heat he felt elated. He saw hardly anything of the others, and although Wayne appeared a couple of times he gave him a wide berth. Maybe he wouldn't have to put up with so much teasing now, thought Jess. But he didn't really mind; suddenly he felt a confident detachment from his fellow workers that he had not felt for the whole month he had been working there.

Jess stared up at the house and felt a twinge of regret that soon it would just be a pile of dust. He hadn't realized how fond of the old place he had been getting. He returned to the bonfire and soon the sweat was running down his face as he stared into the roaring flames.

"You'd better knock off, Jess," said Bill.

Jess was bringing another bedstead downstairs. The whistle had blown and he could hear the clatter of feet as his fellow workers headed for cars and bikes over the broken tarmac of the drive outside. Today they had razed the old stable block to the ground and soon they would be invading the house with their clamour and machines. He thought of Wayne and felt a twinge of intense dislike.

"I'll just finish."

"You worked your backside off today, lad."

"I enjoy it."

"Still feeling?"

"Feeling?" He was suddenly wary again, knowing that Bill was probing. For some reason Jess didn't want to answer his questions; it was as if he was invading some inner privacy.

"The vibrations," he prompted.

"I'll be glad when we get the building down. Won't you?" lied Jess.

"I'll be sad."

"Why?"

Bill looked at him and shook his head. "That fight you were having with Wayne. Did you really start it?"

"I just lost my temper with him. Finally."

"It's not like you."

"I thought it was about time I started looked after myself. Now he won't be so mouthy with me, will he?"

Bill suddenly grinned and clapped him on the

back. "I don't reckon he will."

Don't touch me, raged Jess inside, but outwardly he just smiled.

Between Holloway House and its outbuildings there were dark caverns of courtyards where the orphans had played. One was still marked off as a small football pitch and the other was used as a car park for the contractors' vehicles. Jess often stared down into the caverns from the top storey, watching the shadows sweep across them and the occasional sunbeam that found its way down into the cold well.

He thought of them now and looked at his watch. It was six: everyone else would have gone. Jess felt a sense of relief. He would stroll round and thoroughly enjoy the silence. Leaving the garden, he opened one of the doors that led into the corridor that wound its way through the base of the building and eventually into the courtyard that was marked out as a football pitch. Jess crossed and recrossed the dank space, feeling calm and relaxed. He could hardly feel his body weight, and as he kicked an old Coke can it lifted almost silently into the air. There was hardly any noise as it fell.

He wandered back into the building and in the gathering darkness found the great hall. It was marked out as a badminton court. There was faded scenery on the stage and a smell of paint and candles. The portraits of the matrons frowned down at Jess from the wall. The faces of the women were ennobled, redolent with worthy duty, yet he could feel their warmth radiating down on him and knew they were benign.

Suddenly there was a noise in the gymnasium next door – the noise of a ball being kicked against the walls. It was a sharp slapping sound and above it rose cries and shouts – the sound of children at play. For a while he stood and listened to the game and such a sense of joy suffused him that he was sweating with exhilaration. Now he knew what it was like to feel radiantly happy. The adrenalin was pumping inside him and he raced to the back of the hall where the entrance to the gym was. With a wild cry of exultation he flung it open and raced inside.

In the centre of the floor was a football. He bent down and touched it. The ball was deadly cold.

Jess sat on a bench and stared at the ball, willing it to move. It didn't. The brick was bare in the gym and there still seemed to be a smell of sweat and rubber, but it was dark and cool in the long high-ceilinged room. He looked up to the rafters and saw cobwebs and tiny cautious movements. Spiders. With sudden decision, Jess stood up and kicked the ball. It sagged its way towards the wall until it met the brickwork with a soft splat.

Jess walked back down the corridor. He heard a creaking and knew, before he reached the window, that it was the swing.

The slender young boy was swinging as high as he could, silhouetted by the dying sun behind him. His dark hair flew out against the light. He was wearing a T-shirt, jeans and trainers and his face was wide and innocent, radiant with the joy of the swing. Jess stood watching him through the dusty window. He swung and swung until the swing was almost parallel with the top bar.

On an impulse, Jess opened the door. As he suspected, the boy was no longer there but the swing was still moving. He walked slowly across to it and found, once again, that the seat was deadly cold to his touch. He sat on it and begun to swing himself to and fro. Jess felt enormously relaxed. He closed his eyes and could smell baked beans again and something else. It was the delicious smell of bacon frying. He swung smoothly to and fro and could hear a voice calling, "Come on, Frank. Supper's ready."

My name's Jess, he said to her in his mind but Matron replied "It's all the same to me. You know that I can never remember names."

She laughed again, that lovely light laugh, and he got off the swing and followed her into the house and into the yellow glow of the empty hall. Jess looked at his watch and saw that it was almost seven. Mum would be worried. He must get home.

Reluctantly, he left the hall and walked past the old kitchens. For a moment he could still smell the baked beans. He hurried on, up the corridor, through the foyer with the mosaic tiling and out into the front drive, pushing the main door closed behind him, making sure that it caught on its Yale lock. Then he began to run home.

Chapter Four

Jess made a point of sitting with his mother that evening and together they watched the television. But he found it almost impossible to concentrate however hard he tried, and he was conscious of her glancing at him all the time. He dreaded the questions she was dying to ask and knew that she was trying to hold herself back from doing so. The fact that she was trying not to annoy him was somehow much worse than if she had been annoying him, and he was soon rigid with tension. Jess was also stiff and sore, partly from the flurried combat he had had with Wayne and partly from carting the beds down the stairs all day. He hoped that there weren't any bruises showing and that she wouldn't come into the bathroom, for he was anxious to have a bath and to try and relax. Ever since he had been a little boy she had always come in, and although he had longed to ask her if she would mind if he locked the door, he had never got round to the suggestion in case he hurt her feelings. Mum was so easily hurt nowadays and this time-honoured ritual of her arrival in the bathroom was an intimacy that she still seemed to want to share.

Eventually the serial ended and he was relieved to say, "I'm going to stagger into a bath, Mum."

She smiled up at him and went out to the kitchen to make them a milky drink as she always did at this time. Despondently he went upstairs to the bathroom. Once inside he felt the anger grip him so fiercely that he could hardly breathe, and without any further concern for his mother's feelings Jess snapped the lock on and ran the bath.

He was just beginning to relax when he saw the handle of the bathroom door turn and then turn again. There was a pause and then the handle turned for the third time.

"Jess, the door's locked," she said, in hurt surprise.

A voice inside him that he knew was not really his own replied, "I know."

There was a long pause, then he heard her go away. He was sure she was sobbing.

He was standing outside Holloway House and it was dark. He saw a policeman walking up and down the road and drew back into the hedge. When the policeman had passed, Jess looked at his watch and saw that it was after two. Cautiously, he stepped into the drive, seeing the familiar cluster of the demolition contractors' huts and caravan. The house huddled behind them, looking oddly vulnerable in the patchy moonlight. He could hardly make out its shape as he began to walk towards it, taking care to step quietly.

When he was only a few paces away from the building, the lights flashed on with tremendous brilliance and he threw himself behind a bulldozer. The light was dazzling, so white and blinding that he closed his eyes. When he opened them again he recoiled in shock.

The circular staircase was brightly illuminated behind the big glass windows and up it walked dozens of children. They held night lights in their hands which flickered like glow worms. Dimly he could hear them singing a hymn:

"There's a Friend for little children
Above the bright blue sky,
A Friend who never changes,
Whose love will never die..."

The column of children seemed endless, and the singing was ethereal.

"Our earthly friends may fail us
And change with changing years,
This Friend is always worthy
Of that dear name he bears."

Then, without warning, the light abruptly went out; the singing stopped and the house was once again a dark mass.

Jess blinked, knowing that at any time he might wake up. Then he realized that he was not asleep. A sense of rising panic overtook him. He was actually there – outside Holloway House – with his knees ground into the dried mud. A trickling breeze chilled him. What was he doing there? How had he got there? Jess ran the dried mud through his fingers. He looked up at the pale half moon above him and saw the scudding clouds that raced across its face. He must have sleepwalked all the way. But could you unlock bolts while you were sleepwalking? He was wearing jeans and a sweater. Could you dress while you were sleepwalking? He shivered. What the hell was happening to him? For the first time since the strange events had begun to occur, Jess was afraid. How was he to get home at this time of night and back to bed without waking his mother? And would he ever sleep peacefully again?

Very cautiously he rose to his feet and almost keeled over when the cramp in his leg attacked him. He sank back, stretched out his legs and tried to manipulate his knee. Eventually the pain went and he was able to stand. Limping slightly, Jess looked around him. There seemed to be no sign of anything or anyone and he retraced his steps to the main road. A few cars passed him but, by hugging the sides and keeping in the shadows, he slowly and painfully made his way back to the estate without being recognized. He tried the front door. Sure enough it was unlocked, although he had not the slightest recollection of unlocking it. Very quietly Jess entered the hall, only to find his mother sitting on the stairs.

"I've been out of my mind with worry," she said as she made tea in the kitchen, partly accusing and partly genuinely frightened.

Jess felt deeply sorry for her. There was no hint of his new and mysterious irritation. His old love and concern for her had returned in full.

"Mum, I didn't mean to scare you," he said, sincerely.

"But why did you *do* it?" Staring at him anxiously, she knocked the milk bottle on to the floor. While she was mopping it up on her hands and knees, he told her:

"I don't know. I must have been sleepwalking."

"How could you sleepwalk *and* put your clothes on *and* unbolt the door? Don't give me that." She was torn between anger and relief.

"But I can't find any other reason, Mum. Honest."

"I don't believe you." She slowly rose to her feet, milk-stained and weary. "I just don't believe you."

"You'll have to. It's the truth. Really it is."

"I *know* what the trouble is." She looked almost triumphant, as if for once she had managed to make a decision.

"What?" He stared at her uncomprehendingly.

"You've got a girlfriend, haven't you? You've got a girl."

"Of course I haven't."

"You've been out seeing some girl."

"No." He looked at her, faintly scandalized.

"What am I going to do with you? What would your father think?"

Jess looked at her miserably. Why did she have to bring Dad into it? "Mum – I haven't got a girlfriend. I promise you."

"You've been different." She was stirring at the leaves in the teapot as if they could tell her something. "You've been snappy and not wanting to be with me. Then you lock yourself in the bathroom . . ."

Jess stared at her hopelessly now. There seemed to be no way out. There was certainly no point in using words. He got up, took the teapot away from her and hugged her.

"Mum, I promise I haven't got a girlfriend. I really promise."

"Without your dad I don't know what to do. I've kept you at home too much. I've made you ill." She was speaking very fast and Jess did not know how to stem the flow. "Your friends phone but you never go out with them."

"I want to be with *you*, Mum. For a while."

But she was off again on her guilty tide of self-criticism. "I've been keeping you a prisoner here and now we're seeing the results. You should have been mixing with people of your own age. Having fun. Not cooped up with a sour old lady —" she began to cry "— a silly old woman who drops things and irritates you and—"

Jess finally got a word in and he spoke slowly and reassuringly to her. "That's all got nothing to do with it. I've *chosen* to keep you company, Mum." He paused, wondering what to tell her. "I've probably got a fever or something. I'll go and see the doctor. I didn't mean to upset you."

"Would you?" She sounded slightly reassured.

"Of course I will. I'll go first thing tomorrow morning."

She seemed satisfied and eventually they went to bed. As he dozed off she called goodnight in a tentative voice and he replied, "God bless, Mum. Sleep tight." He hoped that *he* was going to.

"Well?"

The doctor was near to retirement age. Jess had never had much faith in him, and even less since he had misdiagnosed his father's condition in its early stages. Jess often wondered whether Dad would have had a chance if only they had managed to catch the cancer earlier. It was impossible to say, and for this reason Jess didn't exactly hold anything against Dr Lyall; he just doubted every word he said.

"Well, sonny. There's not a lot wrong with you.

You're a healthy beast."

The examination had taken a few minutes and had been very perfunctory.

"Thanks."

"You can dress up."

It was an extraordinary phrase and Jess wondered if he should draw on a feather boa and gaiters. Thankfully he put on his shirt.

"Now what did you say you were experiencing?"

"Sleepwalking." He had only given him a very edited account of his night journey.

"Are you constipated at all?"

"No."

"Have you been sleeping badly?"

"If walking in your sleep is sleeping badly . . ."

"Your temperature's normal." He paused. "Have you tried Horlicks?"

Jess shook his head and Dr Lyall brightened. He was a bit like Mum; he appreciated a cosy solution.

"Well now —" Dr Lyall rubbed his hands. "— how old are you?"

"Fourteen."

"And still growing." He smiled and Jess wondered if he was going to cry out "Eureka". "Of course you're still growing and that's the problem."

"How do you mean?"

But the doctor wasn't divulging the mystery and simply muttered, "Puberty does some funny things to us." He began to write out a prescription. "I want you to take one of these three times a day."

"What are they?"

"Vitamins. You want to be chock full of vitamins at your age. And don't forget the Horlicks."

* * *

Jess phoned his mother from a call box.

"He said I was to take some vitamins. He's given me a prescription." He thought she would question him further but the mention of a prescription seemed to satisfy her.

"That's good."

"I don't know if they'll do the trick."

"Doctor knows best." She sounded vague but reassured and he realized that he should ring off while she was happy.

"See you later, Mum."

"Are you sure you should go into work?"

"He didn't give me a sick note."

"Right. Better go in then."

That seemed to say everything. He was amazed that she could still have such complete faith in doctors, despite the fact that Dr Lyall hadn't been able to do anything for Dad. She was blind. But at least it was a convenient blindness.

"I'll be home on time."

"And you *must* have an early night."

"Bye, Mum."

Chapter Five

"You O.K.?" Wayne was standing in the drive with a wheelbarrow.

The bulldozer which he had hidden behind was still in position, and Jess looked up at the house; through the big windows at the front he could dimly make out the spiral staircase.

"Fine. Been to see the doc," he said, surprised that Wayne should show any interest in him.

They stood facing each other without speaking. Then Albert, a big lumbering and very slow labourer, came up and said, "Wayne - you ever coming with that barrow?" His voice was adenoidal, and as Albert marched past Wayne raised his eyebrows at Jess in mock outrage before he followed him. But Jess could only feel a surge of renewed dislike.

"You O.K.?" Bill repeated Wayne's words as they sat in his office. "You look awful."

"Thanks."

"Don't you want to take the day off?"
"I'd rather work."
"O.K."
There was a long silence while Bill endlessly stirred a cup of tea. Then he said hesitantly, "I want to talk to you."
"Yes?" Jess was immediately wary.
"I seen something."
"Seen something?"
"Something funny. Not funny ha ha."
Jess's wariness increased. "What was it?'
"Yesterday. Before I left. I seen something then."
"Well?"
"I was out in the garden, round them swings like and the light went sort of bright. I got dazzled and closed me eyes. When I opened them again I saw him."
"Who?"
"Boy on a swing. Innocent-looking kid."
Alarm bells rang in Jess's mind. Then a feeling of possessiveness came over him. "What boy? I thought no one was allowed to use the grounds."
Bill gave him a confiding smile and suddenly, irrationally, Jess felt a wave of dislike for him. The visions – if they were visions – were *his*. He didn't want to share them with anyone.
"This boy wasn't real. He was from somewhere else," said Bill, positively.
"Where?"
"Limbo." Bill gave a knowing smile and fiddled with his moustache.
"Limbo?" Jess dwelt over the word, deliberately sounding as incredulous as he could.
"Come on, Jess. You and me are the same. That boy . . ." He gave Jess a confiding smile.

"What did he look like?"

"Pretty up-to-date really; jeans and T-shirt and trainers."

Jess felt a spurt of real anger. It would seem that Bill could see what he was seeing. And for some reason he couldn't really understand, he didn't want Bill to see what he could see.

"I had a dream about you last night," Bill continued. "A really strange one."

"Yes?"

"Saw you in the grounds, here, crouching and watching. And then the window lit up and there were kids moving up the staircase. Lots of 'em." He fiddled with his moustache again and once more gave him the irritatingly confiding smile.

"What were they doing?" asked Jess flatly.

"Going up the stairs. I told you. With little lights in their mitts. And you was watching them and I was watching you. Then I woke up."

"Some dream!" Jess tried to sound light-hearted and failed.

"It were a vision," said Bill firmly and smugly. He stared at Jess as if challenging him to deny it, and Jess wondered if he, too, could feel the enmity that had sprung up between them. It was like a force in the air.

"What are you going to do?" asked Jess.

"*Do?*" Bill stared at him very intently. "That kid shouldn't be seen."

"Are you sure it wasn't a trick of the light?"

"Come on, Jess —"

"But then why don't you leave him be?"

"You don't understand, son. He shouldn't be hanging round here like that. He's obviously in limbo, not able to move on like. I reckon the best thing I can do is bring the missus across." He was impatient now and Jess knew that Bill thought he was being obstructive.

"What for?"

"To help me decide."

"Decide what?"

Bill frowned and began to talk slowly and patiently. "We got to work out whether we need a seance or perhaps an exorcism." His eyes glittered with excitement and the word "fake" flashed across Jess's mind. You do this because there's nothing else in your life, don't you? he thought with sudden perception. And all the original good feelings he had had for Bill began to evaporate. He might be a fake but he was a dangerous fake, meddling with things he didn't begin to understand.

"Are you sure you should?"

"Meddle?" said Bill, echoing his thoughts. "That's what they all say. But we can help these poor souls. The missus and me. They need help, Jess. He's not on his swing for nothing."

"You talked about vibrations . . ." Jess's voice petered out.

"That's what we had before. But now we got a sighting."

There was obviously no deterring him and, regretfully, Jess rose to his feet. "I'd better get on then."

"Right." Bill suddenly looked relieved and Jess realized that the conversation with all its undercurrents, had been a strain for both of them. "By the way, there's a lady coming. She wants to take a look round before we get to pulling the old place apart."

"Who is she?"

"One of the matrons or something. Any chance of you doing the honours?"

"Sure."

"She'll be along a bit later this morning. We'll come and find you and you can show her round. After all, you're the expert."

Was there just a hint of mockery in Bill's voice? wondered Jess as he walked out into the garden and down to the bonfire. He passed the swing where they had seen the boy; it stood utterly still, without the slightest movement. Jess hurried on down to the bonfire. The morning was overcast and the clouds were heavy and grey, but it was still smouldering. He'd better begin on the next dormitory this morning. There were at least another six of the old wooden bedsteads in there, and more elsewhere. Suddenly he felt exhausted and heavy limbed. He heard the rumbling crash of another of the old stable blocks coming down. It was Thursday. Next Monday they were scheduled to demolish the main house and then that would be that. He didn't really know whether he was glad or sorry.

Chapter Six

She arrived at midday and was shown up to the dormitory by Wayne, who stood smirking in the doorway. Jess was at the other end of the long narrow empty space, and as she walked towards him she did indeed look a rather bizarre sight.

"This is Miss Flock." Wayne could hardly keep the laughter out of his voice.

Square and short, with huge pebble-lensed glasses and a myopic way of gazing around her, Miss Flock was dressed in an old brown mack that seemed to come down to her ankles and a hat that looked as if it had been bought in a jumble sale. It was red with a kind of drooping tassel and Jess was reminded of an upturned lampshade. Immediately he felt defensive on her behalf.

"This is Jess," said Wayne, showing no sign of wanting to leave.

The old lady was still bearing down on him with a purposeful, if blinkered air.

"Thanks, Wayne. *I'll* be showing her round."

"Who said?"

"Bill said."

"Mr Langridge to you." But there was no malice in his voice and he winked as he walked away.

Interfering busybody, thought Jess.

Jess shook Miss Flock's outstretched hand and discovered that she was wearing gloves that smelt of mothballs.

"Can I show you round?"

When she spoke, her voice was oddly deep and strong. "Thank you. I was here quite a few years ago, and when I heard that they were going to knock the old place down I had to come."

"You're just in time." Suddenly he liked her, feeling the personal warmth that radiated from her. However strange Miss Flock looked; Jess felt happy and reassured in her presence.

"I remember every inch of this place." She was looking round, her eyes like tadpoles behind the huge glasses, darting into every nook and cranny of the bare room in painful nostalgia. "There was blue lino on the floor. Look, there's a bit of it left over there. Blue lino and twelve beds either side, all wooden like that one. And each bed had a locker beside it and there were blue counterpanes on the beds."

As Miss Flock spoke, Jess could see the room as it had been, and he followed her eyes as she recalled each little detail.

"There was a strip of carpet down the middle – just to give a bit of warmth to the lino – and a big table where we used to have the cocoa at night." She looked across at the bare windows. "We used to have blue curtains at the windows." She laughed. "So it was pretty obvious what we were going to call it. This was the blue dormitory and there were three others, green, red and yellow." She paused and then for the first time looked at Jess properly. "How old are you?"

"Fourteen. I'm doing a holiday job."

She nodded.

"Would you like to see round?" he asked her again.

"It really is most kind of you."

For the next hour they wandered round the empty building. She was captivated by the pile of roller skates, and as she knelt down beside them he noticed that her glasses had misted up. She took them off and wiped them and he realized she was crying.

"You could take one if you like," Jess confided generously.

"Can I?"

"I've got instructions to burn everything. So I've taken home a dolls-house, some models and soldiers, some cuddly toys and other bits and pieces."

Miss Flock suddenly reached out and touched his shoulder. "That was very good of you." She sounded as if he had given her something very precious. "I can't bear the thought of them coming to any harm."

"Do you want one?" he repeated.

She picked up one of the roller skates and tucked it into her capacious bag. "That'll do for starters." She laughed a throaty laugh and Jess laughed too. It was as if they had started a conspiracy.

During their wanderings round Holloway House, Miss Flock collected a baby's bottle, some marbles, a little mirror and a child's shoe. Her bag was getting heavier, and as they climbed down the circular staircase she stopped and sat down.

"Are you O.K.?"

"I'm fine. I used to sit here when the children climbed the stairs to bed. It was a little tradition that we had. I used to sit here and they'd pass me and blow me the odd kiss." She laughed again. "At least the little ones would."

Jess sat down beside her and a great happiness filled him. He suddenly needed to touch her, and when he nestled for a moment against her coat he felt warm and comfortable. She began to sing a few lines almost under her breath:

"There's a Friend for little children
Above the bright blue sky,
A Friend who never changes,
Whose love will never die . . ."

Then she shook herself and Jess moved away. "You must think me mad," she said awkwardly.

"No."

"A sentimental old fool." She stood up. "Come on, let's go and see if my portrait's still on display downstairs."

"Yours?" He was feeling so odd; partly happy and now partly afraid. His head was swimmy and Jess put it down to fatigue.

"I was matron here, you see. For thirty years from the fifties."

He nodded. As they went down the stairs she was still humming the hymn tune.

"I think someone from the Orphanage Board is going to collect the portraits sometime," said Jess. "They'd better be quick."

"So I should hope. I don't see why we matrons should be consigned to the bonfire. Do you?" She laughed lightly but there was a little catch in it.

Once they were in the great hall she seemed calmer. "We used to have some lovely times in here. I can still feel them."

Jess explained about his one visit to Tom's birthday party round the fire and she gripped his hand.

"Then you'll know a little bit of what I mean."

"Yes."

"Here we are then." She went up to one of the portraits. It showed a smiling woman of about forty. Underneath it was another photograph. A cluster of children sat in front of a Christmas tree in a room that Jess recognized as one of the lounges on the ground floor. They were dressed in fifties clothes – Fair Isle sweaters and aertex shirts and grey shorts. "That was my little lot. We had housemothers of course, but although I was in overall charge I still had my own little group. Over the years I had many little groups." Her voice broke. "Shall we move on? I would like to take one last look at that lounge it you don't mind."

"Of course I don't."

They walked on down the corridor with its brown paint until they came to the foyer. There was mosaic tiling on the floor and a big motto in a glass frame on the wall. It read: "In God we place our trust."

"Is there no way they can save the mosaic?" she asked.

"I think Mr Langridge is going to try."

They walked into another room, empty except for a rubber plant that drooped from a polished table on which was scattered a pile of books. On closer inspection they turned out to be *The Children's Encyclopaedia*. Against the wall was an upright black chair and Miss Flock went across and sat down on it heavily.

"Could I ask you a favour?"
"Yes, of course."
"Will you stay with me for a while? I want to sit here – so I can remember."
"Wouldn't you rather I left you on your own?"
"No. sit down. Do you mind the floor?"
Jess squatted cross-legged on the floor, and they sat in silence as the room and its past seemed to close in on them. Jess shut his eyes and felt completely at peace. He would have liked to have sat there with her for ever and ever and feel the warm blanketing silence. But all too soon she said, "Shall we take a look at the garden now?"
He led her out, and they slowly walked through the long grass towards the children's playground.
"Who's that?" she asked suddenly, and he could feel her agitation.
Jess stared ahead. Someone was sitting on the swing which was gently swaying to and fro. Then he recognized the occupant.
"That's Mr Langridge – our foreman."
"Of course. How silly of me. I saw him when I arrived. He must be having a rest. Shall we creep away?"
A little wind trickled over the grass and then became stronger. Overhead the clouds looked even heavier and blacker. Bill was very still on the seat of the swing.
"Hang on," said Jess. "I'll just tell him that we're still looking round." He knew there was no need whatever to give Bill such useless information, but he felt a sudden and overpowering need to reach him. Slowly, he walked over to the swing.
"Bill."
There was no reply. Bill's face was creased in a

smile, but the smile was fixed. Permanent.

"Bill."

There was still no movement at all. Jess turned to Miss Flock. "Something's wrong," he said. As she slowly walked towards him, Jess knew that Bill Langridge was dead.

Chapter Seven

Jess had run to the site office and phoned the ambulance which had arrived at the same time as the police car. Suddenly the garden was full of uniforms as the rain began to spit, and Bill Langridge sat on his swing and smiled - and smiled.

They lifted him up gently, not so gently levering away his hands which were gripped tight to the chains. Then, when he was lying on the stretcher, they put a blanket over his face to cover up that eternal smile. The rest of the demolition squad stood round awkwardly; privately fascinated by the macabre scene, outwardly respectfully shocked. They talked in low murmurs while an older man, Ned, liaised with the police and ambulance men, talking to them in a low urgent voice.

Jess stood helplessly with Miss Flock. Neither of them said anything. They just watched and listened. Then a policeman had a brief word with Jess. He was kind and soft-spoken, reassuring, simply wanting to know roughly what time he had discovered Bill.

After a while the policemen went away and the ambulance men took Bill, saying the police would inform his wife and that there was nothing anyone else could do. She'll have a chance for an immediate seance, thought Jess irreverently, and a bizarre picture came into his mind of her rapping on a table and Bill appearing in a cloud of ectoplasm, complete with a fag in his mouth.

Ned came up to Jess. He, too, was very kind. "Look, young fellow – it was pretty awful finding him like that. I should take the rest of the afternoon off if I were you."

Jess shook his head. "I'd rather go on working." He didn't know how he felt. Just numb.

"Fair enough, lad. Maybe that's the best thing to do." He turned to Miss Flock who was standing quietly, silently supportive. She seemed very composed. "I'm sorry this had to happen, ma'am. Can I make you a cup of tea?"

"That would be nice. The poor man died very peacefully. But it was a terrible discovery for Jess. Would you get him a cup too? Perhaps we could go back into the house."

"Can I make you comfortable in the caravan?"

"No, thank you. I think I'd rather spend the little time I have left in the house, if that's all right. And perhaps Jess could join me. Can you spare him a little longer? A quiet sit would do us both good."

"Of course. I'll go and see about the tea." He left them together, but Jess was resentfully conscious that while he was talking Wayne had been standing a few feet away. He came up to them.

"He had a heart attack," Wayne said bluntly. "Apparently it was pretty massive and he wouldn't have known what hit him."

Miss Flock nodded. "I thought it must be something like that. The end was peaceful. I'm so pleased." She seemed anxious to get away and half turned back to Jess. "I think we should go inside now. It's starting to rain."

"Funny though," continued Wayne.

"What's funny?" asked Jess sharply. We wished Wayne would go away.

"Funny he was sitting on that swing."

"I expect he felt like a little rest," said Miss Flock reprovingly, as if he was gossiping about the dead man.

"But he had nothing to do out here. I mean – only Jess is around in the garden."

"I expect he wanted a break," said Jess. "I was upstairs with Miss Flock."

They turned back to the house, leaving Wayne staring at the motionless swing in the spitting rain.

This time they walked up the stairs to the only partly-furnished room still left. There were some rubber plants and a couple of old chairs and a sofa which still had a bedraggled and dirty antimacassar across it. Ned had brought them up two big mugs of steaming sweet tea with condensed milk and they sipped them gratefully. Jess felt unreal.

"Are you all right, dear?" Her voice was full of tender concern.

"I think so." He didn't really know what to think except that the numbness was going and, in its place, an alarming sense of relief was gradually creeping over him. He tried to fight it off. Why should he be relieved that Bill was dead? Was it something to do with the anger he had felt – the same kind of anger he had felt with Mum. It was as if they were intruding on him and his gathering obsession with Holloway House.

"Have you seen death before?" she asked quietly.

"I saw my dad. He was very thin but all the lines in his face were smoothed out."

"That's often the case." Her voice was reassuring.

"Bill was smiling though."

"A peaceful end."

"Yes." Jess sounded doubtful.

"Why don't you lie down for a bit?"

"Me?"

She smiled. "Yes, you."

"I don't need to."

"You'll feel better if you have a rest. It's not cold and I can put this blanket over you." Miss Flock sounded sternly kind, matron-like all over again. She produced a regulation orphanage blanket from a pile in the corner. It was coarse and dirty but wonderfully warm. She covered Jess up and he closed his eyes. The old sofa was oddly comfortable and a drowsiness overcame him. As he drifted off he could feel the touch of her hand on his brow. It was cool and dry. After a while she began to sing:

"There's a Friend for little children
Above the bright blue sky . . ."

Before she could go any further he was asleep.

Jess dreamt almost at once. He saw his mother at home, sitting on her own, walking from room to room and wringing her hands as she so often did. Then he saw her standing on a railway station. Trains roared past at an alarming speed and she stood so close to the edge of the platform that her body literally rocked with the vibration. He was terrified that she would fall but, of course, was powerless to help her. Then the trains began to pass so frequently that there was no longer a gap between them. They were also going faster and faster until they became a vibrating blur. Still she stood there, patiently waiting. The wind on the platform was tremendous and Jess suddenly found himself in a station buffet, looking out at his mother's back. He was sitting with Miss Flock and they were drinking lemonade and eating rock cakes. His mother kept vibrating to and fro at an alarming rate, and even as he watched, horrified, she was slowly but surely sucked under the trains. When she had gone, he felt Miss Flock's hand on his wrist. The noise of the trains completely filled the interior of the steamy buffet but painfully he could make out her words: "Don't worry. I'm going to look after you now. After all, I always did, didn't I? Didn't I? Didn't I?" The words began to pick up the slowing rhythm of the train and he woke up to find her hand on his arm. Her face was round and uncomplicated and kind.

"You were sleeping so peacefully. I'm sorry to wake you but I have to go and meet my sister. I don't want to keep her waiting. She gets upset if I do. And after what's happened this afternoon, well, I still feel a little shaken."

Jess struggled guiltily to his feet, feeling heavy, leaden, as if he had been ill. He could see Bill smiling his dead smile and he blinked in the soft afternoon light that was stealing through the window. The overcast clouds had lifted and the sun had emerged, fingering its way into the room with a dusty pale sunbeam.

"Don't you think you should go home?" she whispered.

"No." He knew that this was the one thing he did not want to do and his voice was almost sharp. He smiled quickly to cover it up, but she was looking at him with such understanding that for a moment he thought she could almost read his mind.

Chapter Eight

"I'm the new foreman – Ted Thomas. Just thought I'd come in and have a word."

Jess looked up apathetically. The man was young, in his early thirties, but he didn't really care whether there was a new foreman or not. I suppose he's here to chat me up about Bill, Jess thought. He'll make soothing noises and go away quickly with a bit of luck. But he didn't make soothing noises at all.

"It's an amazing place, isn't it?" He sat, crossing his denim legs, looking round with an air of slight bewilderment.

"Had Bill been with the firm a long time?" Jess asked dully, trying to be polite.

"Man and boy. He was part of our landscape was Bill. Been with us since he was your age. Bit of a mystic too."

"He said he was a medium."

Ted smiled. "Just the kind of place for his last days – Holloway House. He could sit here and plug in.

What did he tell me last week when he came over to the new site meeting? Something about some kid being killed on the line. Few years ago now, when the place was still in business."

"I hadn't heard of that. And I've lived up the road for ever."

"You would have been a little kid yourself. Anyway, it satisfied old Bill. Real-life restless spirit, if you see what I mean." He laughed briefly and, for the first time, made eye contact with Jess. "He'll be a great loss will old Bill. Quite a character. Something special about him. He used to lecture me I'll tell you. I started out at grass roots and I spent a week with him – never forget it. We were knocking down a church in London. They'd had a fire there and the vicar had snuffed it. That was another perfect site for Bill. Said he could feel the vicar's presence and all that stuff."

"Did you believe him?"

For the first time Jess warmed to the young man when he looked away and said very frankly, "I did as a matter of fact. Know it sounds damn silly but I was about your age and Bill and I were alone in the church one evening. We hadn't started the demolition, but the place only had a day to live. I think it knew it. Anyway, we were looking at the spot where the altar used to be and a kind of wind – no, really a breeze – started up and all the old bits of paper and rubbish blew around and got mixed up together. We just stood there and the breeze floated them up to the roof. There was a sound – a sort of a sigh – then stillness again. It only took a few seconds and at the time I could hardly believe it had happened. But later on I *did* believe because the memory of it never left me and I often dreamt about it. Just that little breeze.

It was as if the spirit was leaving the church." He looked straight into Jess's eyes and then stood up. "So there you are – mystic Bill the medium." Ted laughed, trying to sound careless and failing. "He'll be missed, and not just by the living." He shook his head as if puzzled by his own words, and then turned abruptly and walked away. He didn't look back.

The afternoon passed uneventfully and Jess spent the time dragging the old sofa out of the lounge – the sofa that he had slept on while Miss Flock sat beside him. For some reason he wanted it to go. He felt confused and exhausted. Once he had dragged it to the bonfire Jess realized that he had just walked past the swing without giving it a thought. He turned and stared at it. There was no wind and the afternoon was completely still. So was the swing. Jess pushed at it. It creaked to and fro and once again he saw Bill's smile. He walked on until he was at the back door of the house. Then he turned and saw the swing still swinging, still creaking.

The estate was quiet, treelined, and the little houses looked docile in the early evening sun. They were all the same. Jess had lived here all his life. Dad had died in the upstairs bedroom and Mum still slept in the same bed. She had not got rid of his clothes and they still hung in the built-in wall cupboards. His pipes were in a rack in the sitting room, his slippers under a chair, a pair of glasses perched on a shelf in the kitchen and his dentures were in a glass that was regularly filled with hot water and cleaning tablets. All these reminders of him had been so constantly in place that they were no longer reminders, and Jess was only recognizing them now because he was thinking of Bill and his grieving widow and wondering whether she would soon sell all his things or leave them eternally scattered around as Mum had.

As he opened the minute garden gate and walked over their tiny trim patch of front garden, the rage seized him again. It was much worse than his former irritation and belonged, at first, to the neat strip of mown lawn that fronted the tiny house. It was absurd. Like a carpet, a carpet without flowers or any other interruption. The lawn was his mother's pride and joy; she loved and cared for it because his father had done the same thing when he was alive. It would only take a single weed to upset her; she tended its needs daily.

Suddenly, Jess felt unable to see his mother and, making sure that she had not seen him, he ran back through the gate and continued to run until he was in a small and little-used park that he sometimes came to when he wanted to be alone. The park was urban, composed of two bureaucratically regimented flower-beds and a sweep of gravel behind laurel hedges. There was one seat and Jess sat down, hoping that no one would come and share it with him.

Jess knew that his parents had been unable to have children of their own and that they had adopted him when he was very young. That was all he knew, and although his mother had once told him that his natural mother lived in London, he had never really asked about her. There had been no mention of her as a person and apparently little was known about his father. An agency had been involved, Mum said, and she had never met his mother and knew nothing about her. He had occasionally wondered how true this was, but it had never really bothered him. Mum had also told him that when he was older he could speak to the agency and get in touch with his mother if he wanted to, although she warned him that it was possible she would not want to see him.

All his knowing life Jess had accepted this information, recognizing that he was in a loving home, and even when he had been grieving for his dad he had never felt insecure or had anything else but love for his adoptive parents. But now it was all changing. The black rage, triggered off so inexplicably by the neat lawn, seemed to possess him and make him question everything. Why had his mother given him up? Why had he been such a damn inconvenience? It wasn't fair. But why was he thinking about his adoption anyway? He'd always been so sure of the family; now he was sure of nothing. His thoughts were jumbled and unfamiliar but they tormented him and his anger rose. Jess got up. Clasping the anger to him until it became hard and cold he returned home.

Chapter Nine

His mother was first to talk about Bill. She had heard all about the death at Holloway House from a neighbour.

"I almost came up. Why didn't you come home?" She was flapping, having spent hours on her own, worrying.

"I'm glad you didn't." He knew that he would have to speak slowly and quietly or he would lose his now carefully-controlled temper. "I just wanted to work. That was all."

"It must have been terrible."

"I hardly knew him."

"But you found him. Saw him." The neighbour, who had heard all this from a local policeman, had been conscientious about passing on every detail.

"He looked happy."

"Oh Jess . . ." She rushed up to him and he allowed her to cuddle him. Usually she smelt good. She had her own particular smell – honey-water face cleanser and Fairy Liquid. But now she smelt of sour milk. She must have felt him stiffening because she soon moved away. He knew what she was going to say next and waited for her to say it.

"Jess, what's the matter?"

"Nothing. Except I saw a dead man. Doesn't happen every day." He had never used sarcasm on her before and she literally staggered back. Oh God, he thought. She's going to be understanding now.

"I'm sorry, Jess. I'm just being selfish. You've been through a lot. I've got a nice supper for you. A fry up. I know you love that."

A fry up? On a hot summer's evening like this? She must be mad.

"Mum."

"Yes?" She was like an eager child.

"Have you started cooking?"

"Not yet. But I can start right away. I shan't be long. Really."

"Could I just have a sleep first?"

"Of course."

"And will you do me a favour? Wake me at nine. I'll eat then."

"Yes, dear."

"And will you lock my door? I don't want to sleepwalk again."

"But I'll be here."

"Please, Mum."

She looked reluctant at first, but quickly caved in. He could almost hear her thinking, humour him.

Before he could say anything that he would regret, Jess ran up the stairs, went into his bedroom and closed the door. He lay on the bed and tried to control the rage that was now boiling inside him. A few minutes later he heard her come upstairs and quietly lock the door. She called out "God bless" and then he heard her going downstairs again. Jess turned and buried his face in the pillow, beating his hands against the bedhead until they were sore.

Later he slept and slept deeply. Just before he woke, the dream came. Or was it a dream? He had got out of bed and was standing by the ruined dolls-house; looking down at the little crib in the nursery in which lay two battered and blackened baby dolls. They were next on his cleaning list but he had not yet got round to them. Jess knelt down and picked up the crib.

The babies were alive, squirming, emitting tiny cries and rocking themselves to and fro. They bawled in unison, their faces red and swollen. Then one of them stopped rocking and smiled up at him. He stared down at it, and noticed that the flesh was coming away from the cheeks in shards until it was a shrivelled mummy. Meanwhile the other baby continued to rock itself to and fro. Jess peered at it very intently until it stopped rocking and lay on its back. Horrified, he realized that he was staring into his own face.

Jess woke and slowly came to. Had he dreamt, or had he really been standing in front of the dolls-house just as he had been standing in front of Holloway House last night? Slowly he rose, feeling as exhausted as he had when he had come up to sleep. He looked at his watch. It was half-past eight. He sat down by the dolls-house and looked into the minute nursery. There was no sign of the crib at all.

Jess drew back; he could feel himself shaking inside. Then he saw it. The crib was on the floor a few feet away from him. He must have left it there before he climbed back into bed. Left it there? He suddenly realized the implications of the thought. So it had *not* been a dream. He had sleepwalked his way to the dolls-house. What would have happened if the door had not been locked? Where would he have ended up?

Jess picked up the crib. It was made of the same kind of metal as the toy cars and tanks that he had rescued and were now standing on his dressing table. The two babies inside the crib were made of blackened lead and they were turned inwards towards each other. He tried to separate them, but in doing so one of the arms came off and dropped on to the floor. Jess picked it up and the coldness seared into his fingers to such an extent that he dropped the lead babies back into the cradle with a cry of pain.

Fear had now replaced his anger and Jess knew that he did not want to remain in his room a moment longer. He began to thump at the door, but there was no response.

The silence was total. Jess kept yelling his mother's name and banging at the door so hard that his knuckles hurt. Waves of panic filled him, and when he glanced back at the dolls-house he saw a tiny black arm on the carpet and he choked. How had that got there? Surely he had put it back in the crib? He knew that he had. Then he pounded at the door again. When he looked back he was sure that the arm had moved another few centimetres towards him. The minute hand was stretched out in his direction. Jess felt vomit rising in this throat and he hurled himself bodily at the door. It didn't move at all and he backed away, accidentally treading on the hand. When he looked down he saw that he had broken it into four pieces and that each piece was moving towards him like a scurrying insect. Soft and scurrying, spider light.

Could he hear her moving quietly up the stairs, or was there no footfall at all? He looked down. The black darts were touching his trainers and, with a scream, Jess rushed at the door, once again throwing his whole body at the woodwork. This time it gave with a rendering crash and he was deposited on the landing carpet with the door hanging off its hinges behind him. He lay there gasping, and in a few seconds his mother had run up the stairs. He looked at her. She still smelt of stale milk and her eyes were glassy and bulging and stupid.

"Where the hell have you been?"

"I couldn't hear anything until now. What's happened? Oh look at the door," she wailed. "What have you done?"

"I'm sorry, Mum."

She looked at him in despair and his heart went out to her.

"I love you, Mum."

"Jess, what's going on? What's the matter with you?"

"I was trapped. The door was locked and you didn't come. I was having a really bad dream . . ." He tailed off, seeing the total bewilderment on her face. Slowly he followed her downstairs and sat at the kitchen table while she flurried round the stove. He remained there, wanting to comfort her but not knowing how to. Then, when he could no longer bear her bustling, he closed his eyes, but immediately he could see the claw-like hand coming towards him. He quickly opened them again to find his mother sitting opposite him.

"The supper can wait. We should talk."

He looked at her in surprise. She was meant to be panicking and crying, not being rational. Where had she drawn her strength from so quickly?

"I'm hungry." He was suddenly childish, not wanting her to get the upper hand – to pry into his secret world.

"Well you'll have to wait." Her authoritarian tone further shocked him. What the hell was going on now? Life kept changing so quickly that he was unable to keep up with it.

"Why?"

"Something's happening to you."

"I'm tired."

"This man that died. It really affected you?"

"No – it was sad. That's all." He knew then that he was going to lie to her. There was nothing that he could tell her about what was happening at Holloway House. He didn't understand it himself, nor the conflicting emotions of rage and terror and love that the place was making him feel. So Jess began the lie. At least there was a grain of truth in it. "I've been worrying about being adopted."

She looked at him in surprise. "Why?"

"I feel funny about it."

"Funny?"

"Tell me."

"Tell you what?" It was as if they were sparring and she was trying to score off him. Their roles had been totally reversed so suddenly that he felt unable to cope. "What's sparked this off?"

"I don't know – maybe it was Bill popping off like that."

She seemed calmer now there was a reason, even if it wasn't a very logical one. He also detected another emotion in her. Was it uneasiness?

"What do you want to know?"

"Who were they? Who were my parents?"

"I just don't know. We went through an agency. I've told you all that."

He stared at her and she seemed to falter. For the first time in his life he realized that she was hiding something. "What is it, Mum?"

"Sorry?"

"What else have you got to tell me, Mum?"

"Nothing."

"But I think you have."

She paused. "There really is nothing."

"You *did* know them."

"No. We *never* knew them." She was very positive. The silence seemed endless.

"What else?" Jess had to force himself to break into her thoughts.

She began hesitantly. "We never seemed to find the right time to tell you before Dad died. I know it was wrong. We shouldn't have put it off. And after he died I couldn't cope with it on my own."

"What are you on about?" His voice was tense.

"You had a brother."

"What?"

"A twin."

"Mum—"

"No. Let me finish. He was in Holloway House."

"No—"

"And he was killed. He ran off. Across the line."

"The railway line? Why didn't you tell me when it happened?"

"Because we didn't know until last year."

"How did you find out?"

But she was not to be rushed. "Your mother gave you up; she thought she could only afford to keep one twin, though in the end she couldn't even cope with one. Anyway, we adopted you when you were a few weeks old. You know that."

"Is this true?"

"I promise. And we never knew what happened to him. Nothing."

"But you found out?"

"It was one of your dad's double-glazing customers. Do you remember you helped deliver to a Mrs Preedy. She used to be a cook at Holloway House during your brother's time and she recognized you as his twin. She didn't say anything then, but she told your dad on his next visit."

"What was my twin's name?"

"Caspar."

"Why didn't Dad tell me?"

"He was ill, my darling. Don't blame him. It's me who should have told you. Me."

"What was Caspar like?"

"I've no idea."

"Where does this Preedy woman live? I can't remember anything about her. I used to help Dad a lot."

"I don't know where she lives now. She moved away to the south coast somewhere."

"Dad must have her old address somewhere in his records. You've kept them all, haven't you?"

"Yes, but it's not amongst them. I promise. I've looked because *I* would have liked to have known more."

"Are you *sure* you've looked?"

"Don't you believe me?"

He turned his head away. "I suppose so."

She took his hand across the table and he made no effort to remove it. "I couldn't have told you at a worse time. That's what happens when you procrastinate."

Jess tried to answer dispassionately. "It doesn't matter. It's just so frustrating. I know he existed, I know his name, but nothing else about him." A sudden thought occurred to Jess. "Why did you let me work up at Holloway House?" Still he felt no real anger, just a sense of unreality.

She shrugged. "The job came up and I wanted you to have some money of your own for a change. God knows we've got little enough of it. It just wasn't the right moment to tell you then. Don't you see?"

Jess nodded. Caspar. Was that the reason he was receiving so much from Holloway House?"

"How was he killed?" Jess asked quietly.

"He ran away and crossed the railway track and was killed."

"By a train?"

"I suppose so. Honestly, I don't know the details." Her voice broke and Jess raised a weary hand in an attempt to stem any more tears. "I'm so sorry. It's all my fault. This is a terrible time to tell you. Unforgivable." Her voice broke again.

"Don't cry, Mum. Please."

"No." And she tried not to.

They sat quietly while Jess's brain refused to function properly. Bill's face floated in. Smiling. Then he realized he was ravenously hungry.

"Mum."

"Yes?" She stared at him.

"I'm starving. Will you do me that fry up?"

"Of course." She rose hastily, obviously glad to have something positive to do.

"And Mum – could I sleep in your room tonight?"

Chapter Ten

Jess lay awake all night thinking of Caspar. The fact that he had a brother was enough of a shock, but the way he had died was appalling. Mum had rigged up a camp bed in her bedroom and he felt reassured by her quiet breathing. She slept feather light, as quiet as a mouse, and never changed her position all night. Towards dawn, Jess drifted off into a much-needed deep sleep during which he did not dream. He woke refreshed, and sat bolt upright, trying to remember where he was and if anything had happened in the night. To his immense relief he realized that nothing had happened at all, and he knew for certain that he had not walked in his sleep. Then he recalled Caspar and the macabre events of yesterday and was assailed again by a powerful sense of shock. He lay back, trying to get used to a new image of himself.

The early morning sun was streaming in through the half-opened window and there was an air of glorious normality. He felt cleansed and the mood swings that had made life so difficult for the last few days seemed to have melted away, out of his consciousness. Slowly he got out of bed and tiptoed across to his mother who was still sleeping peacefully. Thank God the events of last night had not given her a sleepless night. Perhaps they had both been given this gift of sleep. His animosity towards her seemed inexplicable now, and all he wanted to do was to stroke her forehead and show her all the love in the world.

"Mum."

She stirred sleepily.

"Mum."

She opened her eyes and smiled. Then she looked miserable as the memories flooded back.

"Have you forgiven me?"

"Of course I have."

"Really?" She was tense again. "I've made such a mess of everything. Your dad would be so disappointed."

"Rubbish. He'd be proud of you."

"I'm not so sure."

"I'm pleased I had Caspar. I just want to find out more about him. Do you mind?"

"Of course I don't mind. It's your right."

"Would you like a cup of tea?"

She sat up and kissed him. "I'd love one."

He went down and made it and when he came in with her cup she was sitting up in bed in a pink bed jacket that he had not seen for ages.

"Here you are."

"I'm wearing something that I haven't worn since your father died."

"I thought I hadn't seen it for a while."

"I've made a resolution."

"What's that?"

She sipped her tea. "Ever since he died I've stood still. Now I'm going to get going again."

"I'll help you."

"We'll both help each other."

"Will you help me with Caspar?"

"Of course I will."

They sat there silently and companionably. Thank God it's over, thought Jess. Whatever it was. Now we can begin again.

"Will you be going in to work today?"

"Yes."

"It won't make you feel bad?"

"It's over, Mum." He kissed her gently.

She watched him pack up all the toys into two huge cardboard boxes. Even the dolls-house and its contents went in. Then Jess staggered out of the door with them.

"You're right," she called out after him. "I'm sure you're right. All this orphanage stuff is getting on your nerves."

That's an understatement, he thought as he stumbled up the road with the boxes, pausing frequently to take a rest. Jess knew that he very definitely *was* right. He could no longer have the toys around him for they seemed charged, almost as if they acted as channels for something that he couldn't understand.

Eventually he arrived at Holloway House. He looked round anxiously. It would be awful if a laughing, mocking Wayne arrived to torment him.

Jess could almost hear his voice now.

"Brought your little toys back, diddums? Got tired of them already?"

But then he remembered that Wayne was actually

being decent to him. The fight and the fact that he didn't grass on him to Bill had obviously earned his respect. But nothing altered Jess's feelings for Wayne. He still hated him and he cast a wary eye round as he hurriedly darted back into the house and up to the dormitory, there to scatter the toys back into their natural habitat.

"You O.K. after yesterday?" Wayne stood in the rest caravan and looked at Jess with concern.

"Fine," said Jess curtly.

"I want to say something."

"Yes?" Jess stared at him suspiciously.

"Sorry if I took the mickey."

"That's O.K."

"You tried to sort me out good and proper."

"I don't like fighting."

"I got used to it at school."

"Did you?" Jess didn't know what to say, except that he was sorry, but he didn't want to be friends with Wayne.

"Shall we be mates then?"

"If you like." But Jess didn't like.

The morning passed uneventfully. Jess no longer felt any affinity with Holloway House; Caspar dominated his thoughts completely and he kept wondering how he could learn more about him. Tonight he would ask Mum to help him look through Dad's old order books. Surely they would be able to find Mrs Preedy's old address somewhere. Perhaps letters could still be forwarded from there. Failing that, maybe he could contact Miss Flock. She might know about ex-staff of Holloway House and how to contact them. Surely it would not be that difficult to find out.

At lunchtime, while he was eating his sandwiches up in one of the dormitories, Jess heard a step on the stair and, with a sinking heart, realized that it would probably be Wayne, anxious to chum up with him again. But it wasn't. It was Ted, wearing a boiler suit and a safety helmet.

"Jess?"

He stood up clumsily.

"Not disturbing your lunch break?"

"Not at all," he replied stiffly.

"Don't have it with the others?"

"They used to take the mickey out of me. They don't now, but I got used to eating alone."

"They say you've been rescuing some of the old toys."

"Is that O.K.?" Jess wondered if someone had told Ted that he had just put them all back.

"Course it is. Take anything you like."

"There's not much left."

"You're welcome to anything. By the way - we might have to put in some overtime over the week-end. Pay you time and a half, O.K.?"

"Great."

They sat silently and companionably. Then Ted rose to his feet. "You're a hard worker, Jess. Glad to be working with you."

Jess smiled at him as he walked slowly out. He seemed a very nice guy, thought Jess, and the extra money would be useful. But then he started thinking about Caspar again and everything else became unimportant.

Chapter Eleven

The others had all left by the time Jess had finished hauling the remainder of the furniture down to the bonfire. He looked at his watch; better lock up and get going or Mum would start worrying all over again. Tomorrow he would ask Ted to help him contact the people who had owned the orphanage. Surely they would have a list of matrons and their present whereabouts. He felt he could trust Ted.

Making sure that the bonfire was under control, Jess walked back past the swing. Just as he was turning in at the door something made him look back. The swing was moving again and Bill was sitting on the seat. He turned and waved at Jess casually.

"Caspar," he said. "Caspar's around somewhere. Always has been."

Then the swing was empty again and totally still. Jess stood and stared at it hopelessly. Suddenly a breeze blew up and the swing began to move again, creaking to and fro very slowly.

Hurriedly Jess closed the door and plunged back into the corridor. The sun had gone in and rain clouds swept the horizon. The corridor was dark and ahead of him he could see the base of the circular staircase as it ran up to the top floor. Everything was very still, and the air seemed to hang oppressively. It was thick, blanket-like, and Jess suddenly found that he was gasping for breath. He staggered and almost fell, the air thickening by the minute until his breath was rasping. The walls were covered in moisture now and his own sweat was running into his eyes. Dimly he could hear shouting. The fog was in his eyes now and he slowly sank to the floor.

Jess panicked – then he remembered that the lower he was, the more air there would be to breathe. In fact it almost seemed to be flowing along like a stream. He gasped at it gratefully, as if he was drinking water. He smelt cocoa and baked beans and frying and the kind of orangeade that he had once tasted as a child and had forgotten.

Breathing deeply, Jess lay on the floor without moving; the dim sounds increased until he could see shapes coming at him through the fog. The fog was getting clearer and clearer and now the vague shapes were children. He saw himself walking down the corridor. But then he realized that it wasn't actually him but someone very like him. Caspar? He was wearing jeans and a T-shirt. Wasn't he slightly stockier? By this time Jess was half-standing and the mist had almost cleared.

"What are you up to?"

Caspar was only a few feet away from him now and Jess could see that he was very young – only about seven. But as Jess got to his feet he realized that Caspar was looking through him and talking to someone in front of him. He turned round and saw another boy, a few years older. He was thin with very short hair and angular arms and an innocent-looking face. Jess gradually recognized him as the boy on the swing.

The voices which had been indistinct, as if they were being badly broadcast, were now becoming clearer. Caspar moved even nearer. His eyes were troubled and there was something servile about his whole stance. Instinctively, Jess expected Caspar to walk through him. But he didn't. He merged with him and then seemed to reform; as a result his shape became more distinct. Also, there was something less servile about him now. Something more assertive. The sudden thought struck Jess that Caspar had somehow gained strength from passing through him.

"What do you want, Frank?" asked Caspar.

"The money."

"I haven't got it."

"You know what will happen now."

"You're going to hit me, aren't you?"

"No, I'm going to wait. But if you don't get it soon . . ."

Caspar began to cry and Jess felt his pain. It was awful.

Frank was frowning. "I have to do this – I have to have the money."

"I haven't got it."

"Then find it."

The pain eased as Caspar walked slowly away down the corridor. Frank watched him go. It was not until Caspar was completely out of sight that Frank strolled away in the opposite direction.

When they had both disappeared, Jess stood up. He looked at his watch. It said six. Surely it had said six when he last looked at it.

The sound of children shouting and cheering drew him down towards the hall. He could hear the rain lashing down outside, and as he stood on the threshold he was amazed to see about forty children, some on their hands and knees, crawling under and over a homemade obstacle course, while others were standing, watching and encouraging. A man in a track suit stood in the centre of the room, directing operations. The children were in teams and the excitement was contagious. There was no sign of Caspar.

On the opposite side of the corridor were the kitchens, a bare and empty space a few minutes ago but now filled with gleaming equipment. Everything in them was on a vast scale, with an enormous grill, gleaming steel surfaces, a huge chip fryer, a large fridge and a sink as big as a bath. Steam was rising from it and he could hardly see the two women who were washing up. Jess wandered on, not knowing whether or not he was dreaming, and not really caring. The hands on his watch remained fixed at six o'clock. He wasn't afraid but driven on by a rising excitement and curiosity that he could hardly contain.

As he walked round the house, Jess kept seeing outlines of the children; sometimes they were blurred and occasionally their speech was indistinct or discordant as if the power that was allowing him to see the recent past was faltering.

Jess passed a small room where matron, or someone he thought was matron, was bending over a crying child. She kissed his forehead and spoke softly. In another room two boys were playing table tennis and in another a woman was sewing. Elsewhere an old man was operating a magnificent train set that ran through tunnels, up gradients, past meadows with plastic cows, occasionally pulling up at country stations with lead commuters standing passively, immovably, eternally waiting for trains. In other rooms leading off the brown corridor someone polished shoes, and a woman watched children painting at desks. He climbed the circular staircase to the dormitories. There, all was silent, and he sat down on one of the beds that just recently he had dragged down to the bonfire. He was sitting in the blue dormitory and it was exactly as Miss Flock had described it. There were blue quilts and a blue carpet and blue curtains – even the lockers were painted blue.

Then Jess heard footsteps and he froze; Frank came in and lay down on one of the beds. He looked as if he was desperately afraid. After a while he sat on the edge of the bed and took out a letter. He read it through slowly and then read it again, obviously thoroughly distressed by the contents. Another boy suddenly entered the room and Frank hastily stuffed the letter into his pocket.

"Where's the money?" he snapped.

"Here you are, Frank." The child, even younger than Caspar, pushed across the few pennies pathetically.

"Are you going to bring me some more?"

"Yes, Frank."

"Kneel down and promise then."

The child, who could only have been about six, knelt down, and Frank said commandingly, "Begin."

"I promise I will bring you money, Frank."

"Tell me, again." Frank's voice was hesitant.

"I promise I will bring you money, Frank."

"And you know that you're bringing me this money because I'm a monitor – and because you've done wrong things. How many wrong things have you done?"

"I cheated from Jack in class. I took a marble from Sam's locker. I swore at Mrs Lapp. I . . ." and the litany went on, the small breathless voice running one word into the other.

When he had finished Frank said quietly, "Thanks Graham – you'll feel better now."

The child choked back a sob. "I'll never get any more money. I've spent all my pocket money on sins."

"When do you get your next allowance?"

"Not until next week."

"Then I'll wait."

"But I'll never have any money for sweets, or outings, or the swimming pool, or —"

"Then you must stop doing wrong."

"Frank, there are so many things that *are* wrong."

"You'll get it right one day."

"Will I, Frank?" He sounded – and looked – utterly dependent.

"I've told you so."

"Do you promise, Frank?"

"I promise. Now get on your feet."

Slowly Graham complied.

"And go."

The child scuttled out and Frank lay back on the bed and reopened the letter. Then he knelt down and passionately began to pray, "Please God let her live. Please God let me get enough money to let her live." As the flurried words beat relentlessly at the air, Frank continued his repetitive prayer, the words coming softer and faster until soon they were like raindrops in the wind.

Disturbed and bewildered by what he had heard and seen, Jess walked out of the dormitory and down the circular staircase. His curiosity had gone sour; there was something very unpleasant indeed in this slice of the past. Caspar, Graham – how many more? Frank was so strong, so relentless. Perhaps it was this very strength that had created the power. Not strength, corrected Jess as he began to run down the staircase; it was the sheer naked force of desperation. He hovered in the empty foyer, longing now just to go home, but somehow recognizing that he could not walk out on Caspar. Not while he was so upset. He had to try to reach him, comfort him. It wasn't going to be easy, he realized as he walked back down the corridor to the great hall. Already he could feel himself losing touch with the recent past and knew that it was beginning to merge into the present. Sounds were becoming more discordant and the vision was cloudy. It was dark, and Jess stumbled as he made his way into the hall. The obstacle race was still in progress but it was very blurred and the shouts of the children sounded like waves dragging on the sea shore and then receding to some vast distance.

Jess thought he passed Frank in the corridor. He brushed against something ice cold and thought he heard the desperate words again, although this time they were just a whisper, "Please God let her live. Please God let me get enough money to let her live."

Jess increased his pace until he was half running, half swimming through the filthy murk. Suddenly a harsh and acrid smell was seeping into his lungs and clogging them up. Please God let her live. Jess ran and waded and struggled while the smell became a stench and the atmosphere a thick fog that tasted of bonfire smoke. Please God, let her live. Matron passed him in the fog. She was no more than a wraith. Distorted sounds hurt his ears. Was it Frank's anguished thoughts?

Suddenly Jess found himself back in the foyer by the cabinet that contained the model soldiers and tanks. They seemed neatly arranged and the misty glass was clean and polished, but even as he stared at them they began to dissolve. Caspar was standing there. He was sobbing relentlessly, and as Jess merged into him he could feel his misery through to his very soul. It was a dull ache – like holding snow in wet gloves. Caspar, he cried out in his mind. Caspar – I'm here. But the pain was too great and Jess knew that he could not stand it any longer.

He found himself standing on the steps of the house. The air was cold and the rain had gone. He tried to close the front door but it resisted him. The ice-cold wood was sodden and he felt it open again. Frank was standing there, but Jess could see through him to the far wall. Then, quite suddenly, the door slammed shut of its own accord and Jess tripped and fell down the steps, winding himself. He lay there, staring at Holloway House, chilled by its dereliction.

Suddenly, without warning, the whole house was flooded with light and he could see the circular staircase filled with children with nightlights as they climbed up to the dormitories. Frank was in the lead, the others following like acolytes. Somewhere in the middle was matron. She also held a nightlight. In a second, the image had gone and the windows were dark again. Jess looked at his watch. It still read six o'clock, but even as he stared at it the second hand started moving.

Chapter Twelve

Jess arrived home at about half past six, exhausted and terrified. His mother was cheerful and determined, and immediately he could feel the anger returning.

"Would you like some supper now or a bit later?" The love was vulnerable in her voice.

"I'm not hungry," he replied churlishly.

"Oh Jess." Her voice was a wail of concern. "Of course you must eat. However tired you feel. I was going to do some chops."

"There's nothing *to* chops." His voice was scornful, and she flinched as if he had hit her.

"I could do an omelette," she suggested.

"No."

"A fry-up?"

"Want to poison me?"

She flushed and withdrew, flinching again. Jess's irritation increased to breaking point.

"For God's sake."

"Now what's the matter?" Her voice was shrill.
"Please God let her live."
"What?"
He was out of control. He knew that he was not himself and from somewhere deep inside he tried to reach her.
"Mum."
"Jess." She stared at him wildly and he felt the rage again.
"You should be sorry."
"What for?"
"Not cooking something decent." His voice was strangled.
"I'll do anything you like."
"Baked beans."
"Of course you can have baked beans," she said eagerly; obviously relieved to be able to agree. She was like a child who'd been let off a punishment.
"You're going to die."
"*What?* What did you say? Is this some kind of joke?"
"What's a joke?" Jess's voice was so tight that he could barely get the words out.
"Are you sending me up?" She was angry and defiant now. "What do you mean – 'you're going to die'?"
"I didn't say that."
"Jess—"
"I didn't say anything as daft as that."
"Never mind. I obviously misheard you," she said, her anger falling away.
"Mum —" He sat down abruptly. "— I feel lousy."

Jess lay on his bed and closed his eyes. He knew he had said something really bad to his mother, but what? He just couldn't remember. Suddenly sleep reached out to claim him and he felt himself drawn into warm oblivion.

He woke an hour later, feeling slightly refreshed. But there was something – he could remember something happening – that he had done.

Hurriedly he jumped off the bed, opened the door and ran downstairs. Jess paused before he went into the kitchen, still unable to recall what he had said. Somehow he had to reassure her, to make up for whatever it was he had said to her. He racked his mind for an explanation and had a sudden idea. It could explain everything, he thought, would seem quite reasonable to her. At least he hoped it would.

"Mum." She was nowhere to be seen. He looked everywhere and finally heard her muffled and hoarse sobbing coming from the lavatory. "Mum." His voice was soft and gentle.

"Yes?" she said at last.

"I'm sorry. I'm sorry, Mum. I was drunk."

Slowly she unlocked the lavatory door. "What?"

They had a few drinks at work – in the caravan – and started teasing me that I was just a stuck-up kid. I got really upset and had one or two just to show them. I'm really sorry, Mum."

She looked at him doubtfully. "You said some terrible things."

"I don't remember. I've never been drunk before." He deliberately looked as pathetic as he could. It seemed to work well, for she began to cheer up and seemed to want to forget the whole incident. Gratefully, Jess put his arms around his mother and nestled his head in her hair.

"Are you all right now, dear?" she said, asking the now familiar question.

"Yes, I'm fine. Now I've slept it off," he added ruefully.

In reality he was terrified, for although he could not remember exactly what he had said to his mother, he could remember every detail of the events that he had witnessed at the orphanage and the pain that he had shared with Caspar. What on earth was he going to do? And why was it happening? The questions hammered at his exhausted mind. Who did the rages belong to? Were they Frank's or Caspar's or his own?

"Can I sleep in with you tonight, Mum?"

"Of course, darling."

"And I really am sorry, Mum."

She kissed him, and he could see the conscious effort she was putting into being broadminded.

Jess slept deeply that night and neither dreamt nor sleepwalked. He woke feeling alive and good and for a moment wondered whether he had been so tired last night that he had simply hallucinated and that nothing had really happened at all. Yet even if the extraordinary events at Holloway House had been hallucinations, they remained so vivid that he could still recall every detail.

Jess took great care to talk to his mother very normally over breakfast and to apologize again for his so-called drunkenness. A night's sleep seemed to have reassured her even more, and she was relaxed and talkative. When he left he kissed and waved goodbye to her affectionately, consciously trying to demonstrate his love for her.

The apprehension surfaced directly he left home; Jess suspected that if he returned to Holloway House he would have no control whatsoever over events. But his new feelings for his twin were acting like a magnet and he did not even attempt to avoid returning to the orphange. He remembered the anguish he had shared when Caspar had passed through him – an indication of his brother's own pain. Could he really exorcise it all just by finding someone who had known his twin? Well, it was a start, he thought. They could tell him about Caspar and maybe put him in touch with their mother. He deliberately avoided thinking about Frank.

"Ted?"

"Yes, son?"

"Could I talk to you?"

"Come in the office."

It was weird talking to him in there. Bill should have been facing him over the desk, not this stranger. All Bill's things were still around but Ted didn't seem to mind in the least.

"Now what can I do for you?" He was jovial, reassuring.

Jess had already planned to come clean. To a point. "I found out something pretty weird and my mum confirms it."

"Well?"

"I found that I had a twin brother, Caspar, and he lived here. I didn't even know I had a brother."

"Blimey. Is that why you got this job?"

"No. Like I just said – I didn't know." Was he thick or something? Jess wondered. He continued abruptly, "Anyway, I want to find out more about him."

Ted nodded.

"So have you any idea how I could contact one of the past matrons? Is there a list or anything?"

"That would be the orphanage. Not us. But as it

happens, now I come to think of it, your friend Bill got there first."

"What do you mean?" Jess felt a sense of rising excitement as Ted rummaged in a pile of correspondence and then passed across a letter. It was written in a crabbed and rather shaky hand and was not easy to read, but eventually, he managed to decipher it.

Dear Mr Langridge,
Thank you for your most interesting letter. I do remember the little boy, Caspar, very well as I was Under-Matron at Holloway House and later Matron. I retired as a result of the tragedy, for I could no longer bear to work there afterwards and took early retirement. Caspar James was a boy who was continuously bullied and I was never sure why, for he seemed to be an independent sort of child. He was a twin, and his brother had been adopted at birth so perhaps he felt some deep-rooted insecurity.

Actually at this time there was a considerable amount of bullying, although I and the staff all tried really hard to stamp it out. I'm afraid to say that we were largely unsuccessful as the tragedy proved.

Caspar was severely bullied by a sad child called Frank Wilson who had problems of his own. Eventually Caspar ran away and was killed on the railway line. I do hope this helps as I do understand that the passing of your friend - the child's mother - must have made it very difficult for you to corroborate these facts.
Yours sincerely,
Jane Woodham.

Jess's hand shook as he put down the letter. His

mother dead? What possible connection could Bill have had with her? And why hadn't he told him that he was researching all this? Jess's eyes filled with tears and he sat staring down dumbly at the letter.

"I'm sorry, lad," said Ted, leaning across the table in sudden concern. "Had a bit of a shock like?"

"I've had lots of shocks," muttered Jess.

"Did you know Bill had written that letter? I mean – is that your mum he's talking about?" Ted was looking very concerned now.

"I never knew her – it says that."

"Of course – how stupid of me."

There was an awkward silence while Jess wondered whether Bill had written the letter on his behalf – in an attempt to help him in some way.

"Did Bill know about you being adopted and all?"

"Not as far as I know."

"Did he mean that he was a friend of your mum's?" probed Ted.

"I don't think so," said Jess abruptly.

Ted stared at him anxiously for a while. Then he seemed to come to a decision. "Well, you got the address on the letter. She lives round here. It's only a bus ride away. Why don't you look her up?"

"I'll try tonight."

"It'll maybe clear your mind a bit. You mustn't let Bill or this kid Caspar prey on your mind. I mean – you never knew him, did you?"

"No."

"Doesn't that help?"

Jess didn't answer. "Thanks for showing me the letter," he said at last.

"I was pleased to. And Jess —"

"Mm?"

"— You strike me as the impressionable type. If

anything bothers you, well why not look on me as a mate?"

"Thanks, I will." Jess just wanted to get away from him. As he left to start the morning's work he knew, as with Wayne, he would not be calling on Ted's offer of friendship.

The morning passed uneventfully and Jess felt a strong sense of anticlimax. He spent most of the time clearing out refuse from the cellar, coming across a couple of boxes of battered toys that he left in the hall to sort through later. He was interrupted by Wayne.

"More toys to take home?" His voice was listless.

"Yup."

"Could I have a look?"

"I'm going to sort through them this afternoon."

"We still got the old workshop to put the bulldozer through. I shan't be free till later. What about after work? We could have a coffee and a burger on the way home."

"Like to," Jess lied. "But I got to go and see someone."

"Girlfriend?"

Jess shook his head and grinned. "I'm going to see an old lady."

Wayne looked at his watch. He seemed very jumpy and was barely concentrating on what they were saying. "You got a minute?"

"Ted will be round soon. You'll have to be quick."

"Do you reckon this place is spooked like?" Warning bells began to ring in Jess's mind but Wayne was talking hurriedly, urgently. "I s'pose it's old Bill croaking that's made me, well, feel a bit weird like. Poor old sod. But I keep seeing things. Only a glimmer, so maybe there's just something wrong with me eyesight."

"Glimmer?"

"Yes, like when the telly's gone wrong. I see this kid – tall and skinny. And he's sort of – watching."

"Where have you seen him?" Jess snapped and then, too late, tried to be casual. "Anywhere in particular?"

"All over the place, mainly downstairs."

"Anyone else?"

"No. But there's something else. And that's the thing that's really bothering me."

"What?"

"I think he touched me. I could feel a touch. It was horrible. And I could smell him."

Jess almost laughed hysterically but stopped himself just in time.

"He smelt of pear drops."

Chapter Thirteen

Jess tried to keep his mind on clearing out the cellar, but his brain was working overtime. First Bill, then himself, now Wayne. And the fact that Wayne knew made him furiously angry. How many more people were going to be affected by the ghost life of Holloway House? But then he corrected himself. Caspar might be a ghost, but what about the others? The other orphans must be alive. If so, if they weren't ghosts, what were they seeing? Just the recent past? The ghosts of childhood? But then there was the matron – and the staff. Jess closed his eyes. He just couldn't think straight any more.

The whistle suddenly shrilled and with relief he said goodbye to Ted.

"You're off early. I thought you were into mooning about the place after work." He grinned, trying to be matey, trying to extract more of his confidences.

"Not tonight."

"Of course. You're off to see Mrs Woodham about

your brother. Best of luck, Jess. I hope it puts your mind at rest."

"I feel fine." Was he that transparent? "See you tomorrow."

Jess ran out of the house and passed Wayne getting on his motorbike. He looked worried, distracted, and had obviously forgotten about looking at the toys. As Jess passed him he smelt something. He was halfway down the road towards the phone box before he realized that he had smelt pear drops.

She answered the phone immediately and he could feel the tension in her voice. It must be ghastly for her, Jess thought. She was on the perimeter, always waiting, trying to be helpful, getting all the flak.

"I'm going to be a bit late, Mum."

"Yes?"

"I'm going to see Mrs Woodham – the matron who was in charge of Caspar."

"I see."

"I shan't be long."

He couldn't tell from the tone of her voice what she was thinking. "Take care, love." She was obviously being careful not to upset him, and as he said goodbye and put the phone down Jess cursed life and its complications.

Mrs Woodham's house was at the other end of town and it was almost half past six before Jess arrived. The road was full of large pre-war houses that had once been opulent but had now fallen on harder times. They hid behind rose-hung fences and number fourteen was covered in wisteria. There were blinds at the windows, and with a sinking heart Jess wondered if she had gone away. Yet the letter had only been written a few days ago. He opened the broken gate and discovered that the garden had become a wilderness. The grass rose almost waist high and a cat scampered out of his way as he walked up what was left of a tiled path. Tentatively Jess knocked at the unvarnished front door. The knocker echoed hollowly as if there was not much furniture in the house. For a long time there was silence, and then he heard shuffling. A few seconds later a whisper, thin and reedy, came through the door.

"Who's there?"

"Ted Thomas sent me."

"Never heard of him."

"He's the site foreman at Holloway House. You wrote to Bill Langridge, his predecessor."

There was a long silence. Then she said, "I've said all I want to say."

"It's Caspar's brother here. Caspar James's brother.

There was another very long silence. Then Jess heard a mass of bolts being undone and, very slowly, the door opened. Mrs Woodham was very neat. Small, wearing a black dress with lace at the collar, her face was deeply lined, although she was not that old. He recognized her immediately as the matron who had been comforting the crying child the previous day, when he had entered, so traumatically, the recent past of Holloway House.

Mrs Woodham stumbled and instinctively he reached out a hand to steady her. She practically fell into his arms and he smelt warm milk and cocoa. He held her firmly. Her face was turned up to his and there were tears in her eyes.

"Caspar," she began to say, over and over again.

Eventually he managed to get her inside. The house was bare but very clean. Once in the lounge the atmosphere changed. It seemed as if this was the only room she lived in. There was a bed in one corner and a little kitchen range opposite. The furnishings were chintzy and overcrowded as if she had moved all her treasures into this room and had thrown out practically everything else.

"Can I get you a cup of tea?" he asked.

Mrs Woodham was sitting in a deep armchair, looking quite wooden. "You must forgive me. It was just the shock of seeing you. You're so like him. So like what he would have been. Perhaps a little chubbier in the face but adolescence does do surprising things to boys." She was staring at him, focusing her soft milky blue eyes on his face. "Why have you come?"

Before he could stop himself Jess told her everything, including all the things he had seen and heard at Holloway House. When he had finished, he realized the extent of the shock he had given her. Her lips were working and a little pulse beat in her throat. But when she spoke he could see she was trying to be as calm as possible.

"I know Miss Flock. She was my predecessor and I worked under her for a while. She's a good woman but she loved the children so much that she no longer knew or understood them. In fact her love made her blind to what was going on there. I'm not surprised she didn't recognize your likeness to Caspar. She was totally unobservant, I'm afraid."

Jess was relieved. What he had told her could have sounded an extraordinary story of ghostly glimpses and bizarre happenings, but she hadn't laughed at him. His face must have given him away for she smiled for the first time.

"You've had a terrible time." She paused. "But it's no wonder there are so many echoes in that place. It wasn't all unhappy, you know. It was just that Frank had terrible problems and we didn't find out for a long time. He managed to conceal them completely from Miss Flock, of course, and then when I became matron it took me far too long to find him out."

"What happened to him? Where is he now?"

"He's working up north."

"Do you ever see him?"

She hesitated. "He writes. Frank came to the orphanage when he was eleven. His mother had terminal cancer and his father completely rejected him. But for some reason Frank had got hold of the idea that if his mother went to a special clinic in America she'd be cured and he could come home. I think he must have misunderstood something his father said. Anyway he began to bully the little ones into giving him money – and the more he bullied the more powerful and successful he became. He got away with it for quite a long time, and what drove him on was trying to amass a sum of money that he would never be able to collect. But he loved her to such an extent that it all became an appalling obsession."

"How was he stopped?"

She stared at him for so long that Jess began to grow uncomfortable. Then she said, "I found him out in the end, and he had to leave and go to a special school. I think he wanted to be found out in one way. But his mother died and he became very disturbed." She paused again. "I never go near the house now. My husband died last year and I'm on my own with my memories." She gave an uncomfortable little laugh.

Jess looked at her with concern and then he burst out: "I want to know about Caspar. I want to know how he died."

She nodded. "Very well. But when I've told you I don't think we should meet again. Nursing memories like these is bad enough for one. If there are two of us we shall begin to feed off each other." She paused and then began to speak slowly. "Miss Flock was a very good and kind and loving woman. She loved the children and she loved the house. She had no children of her own, so they were a replacement family for her. That was the trouble. It made her blind. She wanted good and loving children so she invented good and loving children. She hadn't counted on Frank's obsession. Your brother must have suffered a great deal. In the end he ran away. He ran across the railway line in front of a train."

"What was Caspar like?"

"Oh, he was wonderful. A lovely boy. Healthy and natural and mischievous. He was a *real* angel. Not that he looked like one. Thank God." She paused again. "He was brave too, and he got into a lot of fights at the orphanage. He was no coward, but Frank seemed to have a real hold on those children. They gave up all their sweets and pocket money to him."

"What about his parents? Our parents?"

"Do you know anything about them? I mean, I wonder if I should tell you." She stopped and thought. "You've become involved to such an extent that I think you're entitled to know everything, but what about your adoptive parents? Won't they be upset?"

"No, my dad's dead and Mum knows I'm coming to see you."

"Very well, then. Your real mother was on her

own, you see, and she was so young that they said she couldn't cope. She was unmarried and had a drink problem and having twins was a terrible shock to her. She managed to get you adopted and hoped to be able to keep Caspar, but in the end he went into Holloway House. We did try to settle him with foster parents, but they didn't work out so he stayed."

"But why didn't anyone tell us about each other? We had a right to know." Jess's voice was bitter.

"Well, adoption is always confidential, you know. No contact with the natural family is allowed and not much information is given. And in Caspar's case it might have been even more unsettling to know he had a twin, successfully adopted and living in the community."

"But we could have helped each other." He was angry now, but it was not the new anger that he found so uncontrollable, just a deep and bitter regret.

"That could well be. Obviously I don't know all the ins and outs of it." She shrugged.

"And my father?"

She looked at him strangely.

"You know I wrote to Mr Langridge. What you probably don't know is that he came to see me."

"To see you?"

"There's something else that perhaps you should know," she said. "Something that I've been steeling myself to tell you since you arrived." She paused and then hurried on. "He was a good man. He came to see me the day before he died, the day after he received the letter. At first, like with you, I wasn't happy to see him. Then he told me a little about what he'd been seeing. He never saw as much as you did, Jess, nothing like, but it was enough for me to feel I should talk to him, to share with him. Before he left he told me that he had asked to be put on the Holloway House job."

"Why?"

"Because of Caspar. He'd been so guilty about his relationship with your mother that he'd deliberately avoided seeing either of you. But he'd begun to regret that very much. You see – Bill Langridge was your father, Jess."

Jess stared at her, barely able to comprehend what she was saying. Bill Langridge? His father?

"I'm sorry, dear. Was it a terrible shock for you?" Mrs Woodham looked drained and Jess realized that it must have taken considerable strength on her part to build up to this.

As for himself, he had learnt in the space of twenty-four hours that his mother was dead and his father had died in front of him. At the moment he could feel nothing. Jess got up. "I'd better go."

"Sit and have a cup of tea. I don't want you to go just like that. Not after all I've told you. It's too much of a shock."

Eventually he was persuaded to stay and they talked in a desultory sort of way while an overriding desire began to grow inside him. He must return to Holloway House immediately. It was beginning to feel like home.

Chapter Fourteen

In the end they stayed together for another half an hour. Mrs Woodham plied him with tea and biscuits. Several times she stared at him in concern.

"I do hope you're going to be all right."

"Of course I am."

"Perhaps I shouldn't have told you."

"I wanted to know." Jess had made up his mind. He would go back to the house. He had to reach Caspar.

At last she reluctantly let him go and he started off up the road and caught the bus back to the other side of the town. It was past eight by the time he arrived at the house and he had promised Mum he would be back at nine. But if time stood still, as before, he would have no problem.

The evening was warm but there was a slight breeze. For some reason Jess's gaze was drawn to the top of the house. One of the workmen had been talking about the weather vane, saying that he knew an antiques shop which would definitely be interested in buying it. For the first time, he could see it clearly etched against the skyline. The vane showed two children – a boy and a girl – standing out boldly, staring beyond the streets.

Jess strolled round to the back of the house and found that the bonfire was still smouldering. The swing creaked a little in the breeze and he sat slowly on the worn seat and closed his eyes. He could feel the tension beginning to drain away. Slowly he swung to and fro and, as he swung, he watched the railway line. Occasionally a diesel train passed with a rattling roar and he swung just that little bit harder. Another train passed. Jess increased the power and, after five minutes, he was swinging as high as he could. It was a glorious feeling. When he opened his eyes Jess saw a fleeting shadow; he looked again and saw a shape developing like a miniature whirlpool. The vortex became clearer and clearer until he could see that he was looking into the troubled eyes of Frank. For a while he could only see the eyes, then the face and the body developed until Jess realized that Frank was standing a few metres away from him. He was looking at the track with total melancholy and suddenly Jess knew exactly where they were in time. This was after Caspar's death.

Jess slid gently off the swing and deliberately walked through Frank. He felt his guilt and remorse and utter misery but he was unmoved by it and felt his own anger and hatred rising. Jess turned to see that Frank was still staring at the line. Then he took out a bag of sweets and popped one of them comfortingly into his mouth. Jess wondered if they were pear drops, and at that moment his anger hardened into rage.

They seemed to stand there together for quite a while, then Frank began to walk back to the house. He walked through Jess this time and once again he felt all the pain Frank was suffering. He didn't drift through a wall as Jess felt he should; instead he opened the door to the corridor and walked in, shutting the door carefully behind him. Jess followed him into the house and up the circular staircase. There was an atmosphere of melancholy as Jess reached the blue room, and he felt his rage against Frank boiling inside him. The room did not seem to be very well charged. The only distinct figure was Frank; the rest was hazy, the past peering dimly through the present. One misty-blue curtain flapped in the breeze behind a rusted and permanently-open window; a wispy blue counterpane lay in mid air.

Frank, however, did not stop in the dormitory, and Jess quickly followed him up the dusty wooden staircase and into the attics. They had been cleared out weeks ago and Jess knew that now there was only a big empty space, with a few cardboard boxes that he had not had time to remove. But tonight it was different. He saw Frank inching his way past a broken rocking horse and a pile of old dressing-up clothes. Elsewhere, the attic was densely packed with old furniture, broken sports equipment and packing cases overflowing with junk. But nothing had a definite shape. Each outline was insubstantial and there was a fog-like substance in the air that made Jess feel he was wading through cotton wool. He could just see that Frank had opened a suitcase in the corner and he edged his way in behind him. He gasped aloud as he peered inside the distorted interior. There were stacks of sweets and chocolates and little piles of money and masses of toys. Clearly this was Frank's blackmail box – his booty, other children's treasures and treats.

Jess could hardly contain his fury as Frank knelt down reverently beside the suitcase. There was a photograph sellotaped to the inside of the lid. It showed a smiling middle-aged woman and Jess guessed that she was Frank's mother.

Jess's anger exploded, and he raced at the suitcase in an attempt to slam the lid. But instead, he went through Frank and fell heavily on to the bare and empty boards.

He lay on the floor, bruised and with his arm hurting. Then, he heard the breathing behind him. He smelt pear drops and heard the sound of quietly approaching footsteps.

Jess turned round and saw him, walking towards him, his face set in a look of hatred . . .

"Wayne!"

He came forwards until he was very close to Jess. The smell of pear drops was intense.

"Doing a bit of overtime then?" asked Jess in an attempt at normality. But the remark came out as a sneer.

Wayne's fist caught him on the side of the face and he overbalanced, stumbling back on to the floor again with a surprised yelp. In a second Wayne was on top of him, pinning his shoulders down with his knees and driving his fist hard into his chest. There was no expression on his face at all now and his breath was coming evenly, his eyes unblinking. Jess felt the most immense pain in his chest and kicked out, trying desperately to throw Wayne off. The fist came down again but Jess had struggled to one side and Wayne missed, crashing his fist on to the floor. He must have bruised his knuckles badly but he showed no sign of pain. Still his expression remained set.

Jess managed to get enough leverage to throw him off balance and he fell to one side, but in a second Wayne was on him again, and they rolled over and over on the floor until they reached the wall. Terrified, Jess exerted every effort and managed to get on top of Wayne and pin him down.

"Wayne," he yelled into his face. "What the hell are you doing?" But he knew what he was doing. Jess had tried to get at the precious suitcase and Frank had entered Wayne. He couldn't get at Jess himself – they had a dimension between them – but Wayne could get at him all right.

For what seemed like hours, Jess continued to hold Wayne down, and eventually he stopped kicking and squirming. "Wayne, you've got to listen," he said more quietly, but Wayne's whole face was still totally blank and Jess knew that he could not. Something in him tautened like a wire – and snapped. He wasn't fighting Wayne. He was fighting Frank. And Frank had to be stopped. Without thinking any more Jess hit Wayne as hard as he could in the face. Wayne jerked back and lay still.

Jess knew that he had to get Wayne out of Holloway House – and restrain him until he did so. Searching frantically through one of the old boxes of rubbish he finally discovered some hanks of twine. He raced back and checked Wayne's pulse. It was beating steadily, so he proceeded to tie his hands and feet.

Just as he was finishing, Wayne began to recover consciousness and started to struggle. But after a minute or so he seemed to give up and closed his eyes. His whole body went limp.

"Sorry, Wayne," Jess whispered, and picking him

up in his arms began to stagger towards the door. As he did so the full power of the house seemed to switch on again, and as Jess manoeuvred Wayne down the stairs into the blue dormitory he noticed that there was no longer any haziness. The beds were filled with sleeping children and the furniture was sharply defined. He brushed one of the beds and felt the ice-cold touch of the recent past. He looked at the sleeping figure and realized that he was staring down at the face of his brother. Caspar looked troubled and was tossing to and fro, his thumb stuck, like a baby's, in his mouth. Sweating as he was with Wayne's weight, Jess still managed to pause by Caspar's bedside and watch him for a few seconds. Then he whispered, "Good night. God bless, Cas."

Somehow, with frequent rests, Jess managed to drag Wayne down the circular staircase. He had never heard, nor seen, Holloway House so alive. Music was playing, a television set was blaring and there was the smell of a fry up coming from the kitchen. Children ran in and out of the foyer as he finally made it to the door. Dumping Wayne down, he had a breather, and as he stood there he saw the glass door open. Frank entered with a woman who at first he did not recognize. Then he saw that she was a younger Jane Woodham.

"Frank. I want to talk to you."

"Yes, Mrs Woodham." The voice was hesitant.

"My dear – you need help. I know what you've being doing – and I think I understand why. Can't we talk about it? You'll have to give back all that money and—"

"I can't. My mother's not very well." Now his

voice was wooden. "You see I have to *pay* for her to get better."

She stared at him. "Frank—"

"She has to go somewhere special in America. So I want at least a hundred pounds."

"This isn't the way to help her. You must realize you've frightened so many children. I mean – take Caspar James for example – he's always talking about running away. We could do a Charity Walk for your mother. We could—"

"No. I want the money now. It's urgent." His face was working and there were hot and angry tears in his eyes.

"I want you to come to my office and have a talk." She put her arm around Frank's shoulders and he went rigid. "Come on, my love," she said, and her voice was very gentle.

They walked on past Jess and up the corridor. Frank was saying, "It's a very nice thought, about the walk, Mrs Woodham. But it's too late, you see. I need the money now."

Jess humped Wayne through the front door and out on to the drive. Kneeling over him in the warm night, he looked back at the house. There was not a light anywhere; a complete stillness hung over everything. Jess looked at his watch and saw that it was only just after eight.

"Wayne."

There was no reply. Wayne's eyes were open and he was mumbling something. The blank look had gone and he was himself again.

"What the hell is going on?" His voice was hoarse. "What the hell are you doing?"

"You were right about being spooked," said Jess

as he began to untie his wrists.

"I left my lunch box in the caravan. I came back and – and seemed to blank out." He was quiet for a moment while Jess finished untying his hands. "What is all this? Why am I tied up?"

Jess began to untie his ankles. "I had to get you out."

"Tied up?"

"Yes."

"Why?" He was on his feet now, a bit shaky but feeling better. Then his hand went to his face where a large bruise was coming up.

"Because you were spooked." Jess sounded very matter-of-fact; almost impatient.

"What did I do?" He showed no signs of incredulity.

"We'll talk when we get out of the grounds," said Jess, looking around him expectantly.

Wayne's motorbike was parked a little way down the road and he sat on the saddle and rubbed at his bruise.

"You went for me up in the attic," said Jess. "Tried to kill me."

"God—"

"Then I tied you up and dragged you downstairs."

"I feel like hell."

"I had to get you out. I'm sorry."

"I just don't understand what's going on. I saw something on the swing – that's all. Why should I have attacked you?"

Jess thought quickly. There was no way he could explain everything to Wayne. No way at all. "I don't really know what's going on either," he said. "But it *is* dangerous in there."

"I'm not coming into work tomorrow." Wayne caressed the speedo of his bike as if he needed to be reassured by some familiar, much loved object.

Jess seized on his fear. If Wayne didn't come in, Frank couldn't use him. "Maybe you should go sick. Until the place is pulled down. The sooner it comes down the better." Jess hoped he didn't sound too glib.

"I used to think you were a right prat," confided Wayne, rubbing at his swollen cheek. "I thought you were so posh that you wouldn't speak to the likes of us."

"You used to take the mickey."

A sudden powerful thought occurred to Jess. He realized that his dislike for Wayne had gone and, because of this, Frank could no longer use the channel of their hatred. But his relief was tempered by one persistent thought – how much power had the hatred generated? And would it really be dispersed by demolition? Supposing the very ground itself was alive with the poison.

After Wayne had roared off on his bike, Jess walked home slowly and thoughtfully. He was still filled with a tremendous sense of relief that Wayne had decided to go sick. But the relief was soon eroded by the knowledge that *he* would have to go back to the house tomorrow. And when he did he knew he must reach Caspar. He had to comfort him. Somehow.

Chapter Fifteen

The telephone box was on the corner of the road near the entrance to his estate and Jess entered it on a sudden whim. He dialled Directory Enquiries and asked for Mrs Woodham's number. They found it easily. He tried to ring her, but for a long time there was no reply. Just as he was about to ring off it was picked up and a man's voice answered. At first Jess thought that he had dialled the wrong number. But he tried just in case.

"I want to speak to Mrs Woodham. Is that her house?"

"Yes."

"Can I speak to her?"

"She's busy at the moment."

"It's a bit urgent."

"She's busy." The voice was final.

"Who's speaking?"

"Frank."

Jess almost dropped the phone. "*Who*?"

"Frank Wilson. Can I help you?"

Jess crashed the phone down and reeled out of the box. Frank? Frank Wilson in her house? There had to be a mistake. His breath was coming in little short gasps. There *had* to be a mistake.

Jess wrenched open the front gate and tore into the house. "I've got to go out again, Mum," he shouted. "Don't worry, I'm fine." And before she could answer he was off. He had to get to Mrs Woodham's house right away – to see if she was still alive.

The bus journey seemed to take hours and it was twilight by the time he arrived. Number fourteen looked even more derelict than before, with its blank blind windows, and the dark wilderness of the garden seemed as if it was waiting for him.

Jess hammered at the door and there was total silence as the knocking echoed and re-echoed. Then he heard the familiar shuffling steps.

"Who's there?" she said through the letterbox.

"Jess."

"What do you want?" She sounded suspicious.

"I phoned you and a man answered. He said that his name was Frank Wilson."

"There's no man here." Her voice was flat and tired now. "I live alone. My husband's dead."

"Someone answered the phone. He said his name was Frank Wilson. He said you were busy and I couldn't speak to you." Jess spoke very slowly and very loudly.

"I've been alone all the evening. I'm always alone. There's no one here."

"He said his name was Frank." Jess's voice broke. They were going round in circles. "Please let me in."

"I'm too tired to see you."

"Please!"

"In the morning, Jess." Her voice was dismissive.

"I'll be at work then."

"Ring me another time."

"Are you all right?"

"Of *course* I'm all right."

"*Please* let me in."

Her voice became even more dismissive. "Jess, go away. We'll talk another time. You're all mixed up."

"Frank's with you," he sobbed. "Frank's in there."

"There is no Frank here," she said again. "You're tired – you're exhausted. Go home and sleep. *Really* sleep. I'm safe and there's no one else here. I *must* go now." And he heard her walk away.

Jess stood on the doorstep for a long time until he had stopped sobbing. Slowly a deadly calm took him over. He was not going away until he had found out who was the owner of the voice on the telephone.

With difficulty, Jess pushed his way through the undergrowth and round to the back of the house. The garden was even more overgrown here and there were brambles and thistles to impede his progress. Soon his fingers were bleeding as he struggled through a particularly dense patch. Eventually he arrived at the back window, and a little further on he could see light streaming through some glass doors. Slowly he crept up and peered inside. Mrs Woodham was sitting alone, watching television. She looked hunched up and dejected but there was no one else with her – of that he was sure. The rest of the house was plunged into darkness and there was no sign of life whatsoever. Jess stood there indecisively. Should he try and break in and search the whole house? Gradually the urgency of the situation drained out of him to be replaced by a sweeping exhaustion. He peered in again. She was still sitting hunched up watching the television, but now a cat had jumped on to her lap and she was stroking it. Cautiously, Jess began to push his way back through the thickets.

The journey home seemed endless. Jess slept on the bus, seeing in his dreams the dark shadow of Frank striding through the shrouded house.

The conductor woke him up at his stop and he hurried home, arriving back at ten to find his mother worried but determined not to upset him. Suddenly all his love for her surfaced and he threw his arms around her, kissing her repeatedly. Then he sat down at the kitchen table while she started cooking.

"I got you a steak," she said. "Steak and onions and chips. How's that?"

It was good. He suddenly realized that he was desperately hungry. He now felt completely relaxed and while she cooked he told her an edited version of his conversation with Mrs Woodham, and how he had gone back there to check on her because she had looked ill and he was worried about her. He didn't mention Frank, Wayne's attack, or anything else about Holloway House. There were no marks on his face, and although his body now felt a mass of bruises after the fight, he was determined not to worry her. He only had the weekend left now – to try to reach Caspar for the last time.

"Do you feel better about Caspar now, darling?"

He jerked his mind back to the present, knowing he still needed to reassure her. "Much better."

"It was a good idea to talk to her. Will you see her again?"

He could tell by her voice that she didn't want him

to, so Jess sounded deliberately vague.

"I might, but she can't tell me much more."

"What did she say about Caspar?" He knew that she was trying to play down her curiosity.

"Just that he was a nice kid but he was bullied and ran away one night and got killed on the line." He brought it all out in a rush.

"Will you forgive Dad and me for not telling you?"

"Of course." Jess had not given that part of it a second thought. He could understand why they had held back, and how she could not cope with telling him after Dad died. He just wanted to make up for all the harm he had done to her over the last few days. He also wondered whose rages had consumed him. Caspar's? Frank's? The other children? There had been so much anger in Holloway House – all caused by Frank – that he reckoned there would be more than enough to supercharge Bill and him and Wayne.

"Don't worry, Mum," he said as she brought him his steak. "I love you. I want to look after you. Is there something good on telly we could look at together tonight?"

"It's a bit late." She hesitated.

"Just for half an hour." Jess bit into his steak. "Just for half an hour to be together. And then can I sleep in your room tonight? I shan't have any bad dreams there."

She nodded, and he could see that for the first time in days he had made her happy.

His mother slept as soundly as usual but, predictably, Jess found that he could not sleep at all. He was terrified of dreaming, then waking and perhaps breaking down the door or, worst of all, hurting his mother in some terrible way. He knew that if he could keep awake then he and she would be safe. But in fact Jess had very little trouble keeping awake, for his brain seemed to be working overtime. Bill and Caspar and Frank and Miss Flock and Mrs Woodham and Wayne and the terrifying figure of a grown-up Frank paraded through his mind in relentless confusion. Sometimes he visualized Holloway House as it was – empty and deserted with a few scattered toys; sometimes he would see it at half-power; other times at full power. He saw Bill smiling on the swing. His father's smile. Bill trying to keep an eye out for him from his very first day on the job. Then he suddenly remembered something. He had heard about the job through a circular that had been pushed through the door. It had stated "Staff wanted for demolition site", and had been typed and duplicated. But supposing Bill had typed and duplicated it just for him? Had Bill pushed the leaflet through the door in an attempt to entice him there? Of course – he must have done. And this would explain all the hints he had dropped. Bill wanted him to pool their mutual ability to see into the recent past.

Even the smallest objects seemed to contain some of the power. It had even extended to his bedroom, for the toys that, thankfully, he had now returned, were imbued with it. He shifted restlessly in the bed and was reminded of the baby doll in the miniature crib rocking and rocking itself so feverishly. Then, just before he fell into a light doze, he saw Caspar's troubled sleeping face, the thumb tucked for comfort into his mouth.

Chapter Sixteen

Next morning Jess was early for work. Despite his sleepless night he felt fit and alert. The vague notion of helping Caspar was still paramount in his mind, but how on earth *could* he help him? There was nothing that he could do to alter the past. But then Jess remembered the pain that he had felt when Caspar passed through him. If he could feel Caspar's pain could Caspar feel his? And if he could feel his pain could he feel his love?

Jess roamed round the garden and then went to make some tea, all the time wracking his brains to try and find some way of making contact with his brother, of telling him he understood and cared and loved him. It was while he was boiling the kettle in Bill's office – his father's office – that he hit upon a simple solution. He would stand in the garden and will Caspar to him. Surely the power would help. Surely he could somehow plug into it.

Looking at his watch, Jess saw that he had another

twenty minutes before the others would be arriving. Leaving the kettle, he dashed out into the garden and stood by the swing. He closed his eyes and thought about Caspar as hard as he could, but nothing happened. Nothing happened at all. Then he looked at the swing. He got on to it and began to push himself to and fro. He swung higher and higher until the seat was almost parallel with the bar. Then he closed his eyes again. When Jess looked up he could sense that although everything looked the same there was something different in the air. Then he saw him coming out of the house.

Caspar was walking towards him and he was alone. He stood in the centre of the grass looking at the railway line. He was dressed in a T-shirt and jeans and his eyes were full of tears. Jess looked back at the house. He knew that Frank was in there somewhere, making impossible demands. He got off the swing and walked across the grass to his brother. As he came nearer he could feel his misery and indecision and yearning to run away, to leave Frank behind him forever.

Jess continued walking until he was right beside his brother but Caspar gave no sign of noticing his presence. Slowly Jess reached out and put his arm round his shoulders. He drew Caspar to him and he felt flesh and bone. The shock was tremendous and the soft flesh made his arm tingle and his insides hurt. Caspar looked up and smiled at him and Jess tightened his grip until he had Caspar in a fierce embrace.

"Caspar," he whispered, and smiled.

"We don't have long," said a voice inside him and he knew that it was Caspar's. "I know that you've been trying to reach me but it won't last for long."

Jess felt a terrible frustration. "Can you see me?"

"A little. It's all misty."

"I can see you. I can touch you. I can feel you. Can you feel me?"

"A bit. It won't last. I've seen things before. All hazy. Men and bulldozers and a man asleep in a swing and now you. Who are you?"

"Your brother."

"I haven't got a brother."

"You have. We never met because I was adopted at birth. Can't you see that we look alike?"

"It's too misty."

Jess couldn't tell Caspar that he was going to die and that there was nothing he could do to stop him from dying. He just clasped him even closer. But to his horror the flesh soon felt less firm and the shape less distinct.

"What do you want? Tell me quickly. It's all going." Even Caspar's voice was fainter.

"I want to tell you I love you."

"No one loves me."

"I do. I know I'm not in your time but I love you. Frank doesn't matter."

Suddenly Jess felt he was gripping cotton wool and the voice that replied was almost indistinct.

"Frank is everywhere."

"No. Frank is nothing," Jess yelled, then realized that he was grasping thin air. Tears poured down his face as he shouted back at the house, "Frank is nothing!" A rush of air filled the space and he heard the swing begin to creak. He saw it rising and falling, swinging higher and higher, but now he was alone.

"What the hell were you doing?" The voice shocked him back into normality and Jess hurriedly tried to wipe away his tears. It was Ted, striding towards him over the grass. "Taking some exercise, were you? I've been watching you clutching thin air and wrestling with nothing. What is it? Those Canadian exercises or something?"

"Yeah, I was just trying them out." He turned away from Ted and wiped his eyes again.

"You look all in," said Ted.

"I'm O.K."

"Want to take the day off?"

"No thanks."

Ted looked at him curiously. "You're taking this job too seriously, working on your own too much. Wayne doesn't seem to be in this morning. Would you like to help me knock down that old hut over there?"

Jess nodded. He would like to knock something down.

Jess knocked down the wooden hut with a mallet and a good deal of satisfaction. Despite Ted's companionship the morning passed slowly, and at lunchtime he took his sandwiches and went up to the blue dormitory. He sat down where he thought Caspar's bed had been, closed his eyes and willed him to appear. Nothing happened at all; there wasn't even a wisp, a fragment of the past.

In the afternoon, evading Ted, he roamed the house, searching for any more redundant objects that could be burnt. It was when he was back in the blue dormitory that he found the model horse behind a radiator. Made of lead, it was quite large and had a saddle. Two of its legs had broken off, but otherwise it was intact. Jess held the horse up to the light and saw the very faint name scratched across the saddle.

It could have been scratched with a pin it was so faint: Caspar. Immediately he saw the name Jess felt the horse give a faint tremor and he found himself once again looking at his brother's sleeping form; this time he was so faint that he was no more than the dimmest of shadows. But he could hear his breathing and sense his restless sleep.

Placing a gentle hand on the faint suggestion of his brother's shoulder he squeezed it, reassuringly. Jess felt Caspar's hand reach out and he was gently grasped by the hot and moist flesh. He held it for some moments and gently whispered over and over again, "Caspar. I love you. Caspar. I love you." As Caspar totally faded, Jess found himself stroking thin air and whispering to no one.

The rest of the afternoon passed without incident, but Jess was longing for the others to go and to be left on his own for a final walk round the rooms. Tomorrow they would start the final demolition and, by the end of the week, everything would be gone. Now that he'd guessed that Bill – his father – had deliberately sought him out so that they could both contact Caspar, he realized something else. It explained why a clearance firm hadn't been employed to get rid of the old toys and beds and sports equipment. Perhaps Bill had somehow swung it so that it could be Jess's job.

Tonight would probably be his last chance of contacting Caspar. But had he used up all the available power? Could it be summoned again? he wondered. Could it be strengthened? Jess had a sudden thought. The swing seemed the most powerful channel.

He went outside and sat on it but nothing

happened, even though he spent over ten minutes willing contact. Disappointed and frustrated, Jess returned to the dormitory. If the swing didn't work and the toys only produced faint recall then the power must be at its weakest. And whether that was now a permanent state or not he did not know.

He began to scour the building, searching through each room in turn, determined to find some fresh channel – one that had not been burnt out. Up in the attic, he poked into all the cracks and crevices. Then he went through the box of broken toys, laying them out on the floor. He had never looked at these before. There were some old picture books, broken toys, a few battered animals, some more soldiers and a book called *Sunshine Hours Scrapbook*. He picked it up apathetically, and then began to turn the pages with more interest. Someone had pasted in bits of coloured paper with poems and messages on them. The first page had a childish drawing of a woman's face and then lots of little stick people all round it. The carefully printed and coloured lettering read: "My mum is the best mum in the whole wide world."

Jess's hand trembled. There was not much doubt about whose scrapbook this was. He turned the pages. There were more pictures and drawings and then a long poem, part of which read:

"Mum might go to Heaven
I would like to join her there
But if she goes to America
We don't have to fear.
Mum will get well again
And will want me back!
When I'm home again
With my Mum

I'll never roam no more
We'll stick together
Like peas in a pod."

As he held the book, Jess felt the power coming back.

The frustration boiled in him as he strode down the attic stairs, yelling out Caspar's name. The house was gradually forming around him and he didn't know where to start looking; but instinct drove him on. He *must* find Caspar. Walking through the dormitories he eventually reached the head of the circular staircase. With a thrill of expectancy he saw Caspar standing below him. He was very clearly formed, and for once he was smiling. Jess was just about to shout his name again when he tripped and fell. Out of control, he bumped and rolled his way down one flight of stairs, crashing his head against one of the stone banisters as he fell. Temporarily dazed, he sat up and saw Caspar still standing below him. Shakily he staggered to his feet and shouted, "I love you. I love you!"

Jess went on yelling the words as he ran down the remaining stairs as fast as he could. But on the last circular flight he saw that Caspar was fading, and by the time he reached the bottom he had disappeared. With a cry of misery Jess charged through the door and out into the front garden. The afternoon was still and hot and he stood shivering and panting.

Chapter Seventeen

"You going to have a final look round?" asked Ted, as he prepared to leave.

"The last time." Jess tried to smile but the events of the late afternoon had brought an even deeper yearning to see his brother.

"You'll be out of a job soon."

"It'll be time to go back to school."

"Enjoyed working here?"

"Yes. Except for Bill."

"Rotten business that. But the end was peaceful."

I hope so, thought Jess.

At last Ted went and Jess was left alone. Once again he wandered the familiar corridors, trying to feel the heartbeat of the house. Maybe if he stayed here long enough the power would regenerate. Earlier he had phoned Mum and told her that he had met a friend and would be going to the cinema. She seemed delighted, and he rang off with a sense of relief. If necessary he could always ring her later and say that he was spending the night with the same fictitious friend. She might swallow that too.

While the light remained, Jess sat in the garden and finished the sandwiches he hadn't had time to eat for lunch. The evening was warm and very still. After he had finished eating, Jess sat on the swing and gently rocked himself to and fro and thought of Caspar. But nothing happened.

With growing impatience, Jess continued to swing. Bill had died in this swing. His father had died in his swing. Their father. Surely the swing was possessed with the power he needed so desperately. He swung a little harder and closed his eyes. When he opened them again he saw something move by the door of the house. It was Caspar. But there was someone with him: Frank. Their bodies were shadowy and insubstantial, and he could only dimly hear their voices whispered on the breeze.

"I'm not giving you any more."

"You must."

"You're nothing, Frank. Nothing."

"I'll hurt you." Frank was advancing on Caspar, and Jess could see that his fists were bunched together. He had never seen any evidence of Frank's physical power before. He looked at the slender arms and willowy figure and yet – he could feel the threat, sense his brother's fear.

Frank continued to advance and Caspar backed away. Then he began to run and Frank chased him, their insubstantial bodies like smoke in the summer evening. Suddenly Jess realized that his brother was heading for the railway line.

Jess ran hard until he was a few metres behind them. He saw Caspar running up the embankment and Frank standing still. Their voices were faint in the warm air.

"You won't get away over there. You won't."

As he scrambled past him, Jess could see Frank a little more clearly. He was standing, arms akimbo, his face full of alarm.

"Stop," he screamed. "Caspar, I didn't mean it." Frank began to cry.

A little breeze fanned Jess's face and on it he could smell pear drops and misery, and the salt of tears.

Caspar hesitated and suddenly Frank stopped crying. He half laughed, as if to reassure himself that Caspar was not, after all, going to run across the line. He began to chant, "Cry baby, cry. Cry baby, cry."

Caspar still hesitated and Jess desperately began to climb the embankment. He could hear the train coming.

"Bye, baby bunting
Father's gone a-hunting
Mother's gone a-milking
Sister's gone a-silking
Brother's gone to buy a skin
To wrap the baby bunting in."

Frank went on chanting as Jess reached the top. The train was very near now and he could see the diesel locomotive coming round the bend. Then he saw that Caspar was on the track and that Frank was silent.

Jess lunged forward; he was only centimetres away from his brother now but his hand met freezing cold air. Instinctively he knew there was nothing he could do. The train was only yards away.

"I love you," he shouted. "I love you, Cas."

In a split second Jess saw the wraith-like shape of Caspar lying across the track. I'm out of time, he kept saying to himself. There's nothing I can do. I'm out of time. But he kept calling, "I love you, Cas. I love you."

Suddenly, unexpectedly, Caspar turned to him and smiled. Then the train came roaring past and the cold air was gone. So was Caspar. When Jess looked at the track again he could only see a wisp of smoke. Then there was a whisper on the wind: "I love you."

Slowly Jess retraced his steps down the embankment and into the garden. He was sure he had seen Caspar for the last time.

Jess sat on the swing, waiting for the sun to go down. He swung as hard as he could but nothing happened. He swung again, closed his eyes and opened them. Frank was standing on the lawn, staring at the railway line. He was very distinct and he was sobbing.

Caspar has gone, Jess thought, but Frank is still here. Somewhere he has grown up and is still alive. Somewhere he must recall so vividly what happened. He remembered the man on the phone: "This is Frank Wilson. She's too busy to speak to you." He peered into the still smouldering bonfire and wondered if the demolition would be enough. Perhaps the ground would have to be cleansed. By fire? Frank wasn't a ghost, he was alive. Was it possible to exorcise the ghost of childhood?

Jess walked back into the house. It was dark now and he decided to walk the corridors for the last time. Thin strands of early moonlight shafted in through the broken windows and there was a gentle stirring as the night breeze scattered old paper in the corridor. He wandered into the hall, realizing that he had forgotten to take down the pictures of the matrons.

Someone from the old Board of Governors would be calling for them tomorrow morning. There was a ladder on the stage, so he dragged it down and slowly, laboriously, unhooked each picture.

Then Jess sat on the stage and closed his eyes, smelling the mixed scents of floor polish and old gym shoes. The by now familiar smell of Holloway House. Suddenly he felt exhausted, and the bare boards of the stage were soft and yielding. Someone was stroking his brow and Jess slept.

"I'll hurt you," said the voice. "I'll hurt you."

Jess tossed and turned, feeling pain and fear and the desire to run, to put Holloway House as far behind him as he possibly could. He knew that if he ran out of the front door he would be caught, but suppose he ran out at the back over the railway line. They couldn't catch him then.

"Bye baby bunting
Father's gone a-hunting"

He was running through the house and, behind him, the football bounced down the corridor, higher and higher, nearer and nearer.

"Mother's gone a-milking
Sister's gone a-silking"

The voice was sing-song, clipped and menancing. Jess ran on.

"Brother's gone to buy a skin"

The football grazed his back. It felt as if it was made of lead.

"To wrap the baby bunting in."

He was outside now, running across the lawn, and Frank was on the swing, swinging higher and higher. Then Jess was up on the embankment. He could hear the train in the distance and he could smell the rushing, oily, death-dealing wheels.

The impact round his legs was like a wire band and Jess fell, sliding back down the embankment with someone's arms locked round his legs. He landed on the lawn, struggled, turned and realized that Wayne was dragging him to his feet.

"Get out. Get out of the grounds."

"I can't."

"You must." And Wayne began to propel Jess across the lawn. Suddenly everything went beserk. The swing swung on its own but over and over its bar in huge and terrifying arcs. Every door in the house opened and closed and opened and closed again. The noise was dreadful. Children laughed and cheered, lights came on and went out repeatedly until they were both half blinded. Suddenly the air was full of song:

"Little deeds of kindness
Little words of love
Make our earth an Eden
Like the Heaven above
So our little errors
Lead the soul away
From the paths of virtue
Into sin to stray."

The words pulled at them, but Wayne pulled harder

and in a few seconds they were back in the house, running up the corridor towards the main entrance. Doors opened and banged shut, a football bounced down the corridor and they flattened themselves against the wall to avoid it, a broken picture of the stag at bay revolved round and round, a duster and some rags floated in mid air and the chorus of children's voices still sang lustily.

As Jess and Wayne reached the front door, it slammed shut in their faces and, try as they might, it would not open. They hurled themselves at the thick wood, kicking it until they were bruised and defeated.

"There's a big broken window in the old office," yelled Wayne. "Let's go through that."

They raced back down the corridor. A kitchen knife zinged through the air followed by a broken plate, a sieve and two glasses. Somehow they managed to dodge them and continued to race on. The football bounced towards them at an impossibly lethal speed. Faces were pressed against the windows and Jess could see that dozens of children were clustered in the dark courtyard. They held night lights and they were laughing happily.

They raced on and eventually found themselves outside matron's office. The door slammed shut but Jess was able to drag it open.

"The power must be on the blink," he shouted to Wayne.

The office was furnished with armchairs covered neatly with antimacassars. There were lamps on the tables, a couple of rubber plants and a window that led on to a glorious front garden. But everything was growing misty and Jess could see that now the window was broken.

Jess and Wayne hurled themselves through the

empty space and on to the muddy grass. They lay there panting until the door of Holloway House opened and a figure stood silhouetted against the light. It was Frank. The circular staircase, visible through the window behind him, was momentarily lit up and they could see the children filing up to bed. Frank stood in the doorway for a minute or so and then he faded away.

They walked down the road towards Wayne's motorbike. When they reached it they stopped and stared at it numbly.

"He'll be there," said Wayne. "Whoever he is, he'll still be there when the house has gone." He looked round at the rows of neat surburban houses that lined the road. "They're going to build more of these. He'll be in one of them. It'll start happening all over again. It's the ground. He's poisoned it."

Jess nodded. Maybe Wayne was right. He'd been thinking about that himself.

"There's only one thing that could drive him away, that could cleanse the ground, and that's a fire," he said reflectively.

"Still," said Wayne, "I'm not prepared to be an arsonist – not even to get rid of that brute." And he mounted his bike, kicked it into life and roared off without saying goodbye.

Chapter Eighteen

On the way home, Jess decided to phone Jane Woodham. This time he got straight through to her.

"I hope you don't mind me calling again."

"No, Jess. I don't mind." She sounded resigned but very patient.

Suddenly he didn't know how to begin. "It's been awful," he said.

"When will they start knocking the house down?"

"Tomorrow."

"Then it will soon be over."

"My mate Wayne says not."

"Oh?"

"He says the ground is poisoned."

"What rubbish!" she said sharply.

"Frank must have wanted to help his mother so much. That's why he went on doing it, didn't he?"

"Of course he wanted to help her." Her voice was gentle again now. "And we all tried to help him. But it was too late for your brother. I'll always blame myself for his death. We just didn't see the problem quickly enough."

"But it's his hatred that's at the root of it all, isn't it?"

"Hatred?"

"He hated everyone – everything – for letting her die. That's why he's so powerful. I'm sure of it now. Wayne and I used to hate each other and that's how he latched on to us. Frank uses hate as a kind of channel, doesn't he? It was the same with my mother. Directly I brought the old toys into the house he was able to use my irritation with her."

"Jess—"

"And I suppose—"

The pips went and he had to put in another ten pence.

"Sorry I didn't catch—"

"I wanted to ask you a question."

"Very well, but this must be the last one, Jess. I don't want to talk about this any more."

"It's just this. Fire came into my mind."

"Fire!"

"I wondered – do you think it would help if we burnt the land after the house was demolished?"

"Are you mad?"

"I thought – fire might cleanse it somehow," he stuttered, suddenly wondering if she was right.

"Frank is *alive*, Jess, and anyway he wasn't all bad. He had very quick reactions and could be an effective leader. For instance one firework night we could have had a real tragedy. The children in the blue dormitory were fooling about and someone put a banger in a wastepaper basket. It went off and started a little fire. Frank heard all the screaming and went in, put a blanket over it and stamped it out. Then he called me.

Caspar was in a terrible state; he kept thinking the house would burn down. We were very grateful to Frank."

"Thanks for telling me," said Jess stiffly, finding it hard to see this other side to Frank.

"Let me tell you something else. I don't agree with your friend. The atmosphere in that house is so charged with the past that it's no wonder it gave you hallucinations. But once those walls are down, that's it. Now I must go. Please don't ring again." She put the phone down abruptly. Jess wondered if she was alone in the house.

When Jess got home, he kissed his mother and made her a cup of tea. Then he went upstairs and lay on his bed. Half an hour later, he was just drifting off when there was a knock at his bedroom door.

"Yes, Mum?"

"Can I come in?"

"Sure."

She came in looking anxious, and he knew that he must have communicated something of his own tension without saying anything at all.

"Are you all right?"

"I'm fine. I was just thinking of having an early night."

"You've got a bruise on your face and you've cut your finger."

"Work."

"They haven't been bullying you again, have they?"

"Not now."

"Are you going to sleep *here* tonight. Not with me?"

"I'll be fine here. I feel really tired tonight."

"What about the sleepwalking?"

"What about it?" He felt a slight irritation, but was immediately sorry for snapping as he could see that she was already feeling hurt. "Sorry, Mum," he said quickly. "I'll have a good night's rest here. I'm sure sleepwalking's a thing of the past."

She stared at him and he guessed that she did not believe a word he was saying. Was it so very obvious? But he was determined not to take her into his confidence. How could he anyway? It would take hours to explain it all and she'd definitely think he'd gone completely mad.

"Shall I lock the door?"

"No need."

"Jess."

"Yes?"

"I'm so worried about you."

He tried to appease her. "Look, Mum, shall I go back to the doctor in the morning?"

"Would you?" She brightened immediately. "I'm sure you need a complete check-up. Those vitamins just aren't enough."

"I promise."

She bent over and kissed him. "That's funny."

"What's funny?" The irritation was back in his voice, but he didn't think she had noticed.

"You smell of pear drops," she said. "I never knew you liked pear drops."

Chapter Nineteen

The phone call came at about ten. It was Wayne.

"Yes?"

"I looked up your number in the book." He sounded worried.

"Yeah. What do you want?"

"I was just going down The King and Queen and I saw a light in the house. It looked like a torch. I reckon someone's prowling about from room to room. I'm going in to take a look. You coming?"

"No."

"Why not?"

"We could get hurt."

"Well, I'm still going in."

"Wait – I'll come. But let's meet round the back. Do you know the way?"

"Sure, I'll see you in ten minutes. And don't go in without me."

"No need to worry about that," said Jess.

Checking that his mother was asleep in front of the

telly, Jess left a note for her: "Gone to get some chips. Couldn't sleep. Back soon. Don't worry." He closed the door softly behind him and hurried down to the end of the estate and into the wood that eventually led to the railway line. He had never been very keen about walking through this wood. It was a dead kind of place with mounds of litter and the corpses of cats. It also smelt acrid, and as he walked through its gaunt trees and stunted bushes he felt wary, anxious to meet up with Wayne as soon as possible.

As he burst out of the trees he saw Wayne crouched down by the railway line. He was wearing dark clothes and looked as pleased to see Jess as Jess was pleased to see him.

"O.K.?"

"Fine. Let's go."

They carefully crossed the railway line and then ducked down into the grounds of Holloway House.

"Where shall we go in?"

"Bottom of the corridor."

They entered the corridor with trepidation, but there was no sound and no one in sight. Neither had a torch, but Jess knew the corridors so well that he was unlikely to stumble. Wayne followed him, breathing heavily and sending out waves of suppressed agitation. They turned the corner into the hall and stopped dead.

Someone was standing on the stage.

They froze, quite unable to move, then Wayne slowly turned.

But before he could start running the man on the stage whispered, "Stay."

The voice was vaguely familiar. Who the hell was it? Then a searingly-cold chill struck Jess.

"It's Frank," he said.

There was a little whimper of fear from Wayne but neither of them seemed able to run away. It flashed through Jess's mind that he now understood the old cliché about being rooted to the spot.

"What do you want?" Jess's voice was shrill. This must be the man he had spoken to on the phone at Mrs Woodham's. What the hell was he doing here? Then he shook himself. But of course he would be here. Boy and man he was Frank Wilson.

"I know who you are," said the man on the stage. "You see – I have dreams too."

They stared back at him and Wayne let out another little whimper of fear.

"I'm not going to hurt you," he whispered. "I left the child Frank behind." He sounded confiding – as if he were talking to old friends.

"What are you on about?" Wayne's voice broke.

"I'm flesh and blood. Come over here." He did not raise his voice at all.

Slowly they walked across the floor towards him. He was young, eighteen perhaps, and he was dressed in dark trousers and an open-necked shirt. He was very pale now but his face was still Frank's.

"It isn't safe here," he said. "The poison's still here. If something very bad happens in a place or a building it leaves its mark. You've experienced that. Both of you."

"Have you been living at Mrs Woodham's?" asked Jess.

"She took me in." He paused. "I'm on my own and out of work. But ever since I came back this place has been reaching out to me, trying to suck me in. Tonight I had to come."

There was a very long silence and Jess felt the fear screaming inside him.

"Mrs Woodham," he choked out. "Have you hurt Mrs Woodham?"

"Why should I hurt her? She's my friend. My *only* friend."

Jess could feel Wayne trembling and he put what he hoped was a reassuring hand on his arm. He wanted to go on talking to Frank.

"You killed my brother."

"I frightened him into it. Don't think it hasn't stayed with me for the rest of my life. It's why I'm here now."

"Rush him. He's a nutter," yelled Wayne suddenly, with a burst of unexpected courage, but Jess held him back.

"Wait. Just wait." He turned back to Frank. "Why have you come here?"

"I want to burn him out. Eradicate him completely."

"He's you," said Jess aghast.

"He's poison. His cruelty – it poisoned the house. And it was all for nothing," he added bitterly.

"The ground, too?" asked Wayne, trying to recall the man to the present.

Without replying, Frank began to walk down from the stage towards them. Wayne edged nearer to Jess. It was a good feeling. They both knew they were going to protect each other.

"I want to burn this place. I want to burn *him*." Frank looked round wildly, as if he was expecting to see his childhood confronting him.

"You can't do that," said Jess.

"Come on. Let him do it." Wayne began to walk away, dragging Jess with him. "Come on," he repeated, but Jess shrugged him off. They looked back and saw that Frank was once more on the stage and was unscrewing a can of petrol. "Come on," said Wayne for the third time, but now they could hear the bouncing in the corridor and saw the football coming towards them. Slowly at first and then with renewed strength. The house was defending itself. A door slammed and Jess was sure that he could hear children singing.

"The house will fight you," warned Jess. "It won't let itself be burnt down. Not just like that."

But Frank was not listening. "I can hear him," he said. "I can hear him."

Footsteps began to resound down the corridor and a voice yelled, "You've got to give it to me. I need it for my mother."

"He's going to meet himself," screamed Wayne. "We can't see this."

Jess knew they couldn't, and they both turned and ran towards the garden door at the end of the corridor. As they ran the door tried to slam in their faces, but Wayne held on to it and they managed to squeeze through.

"Don't look back," shouted Wayne, but Jess couldn't stop himself. He saw the young Frank walking down the corridor and the man Frank come out to greet him. The smell of petrol was intense as they merged into one another. Then they heard the striking of a match.

The swing creaked as they passed it and the old iron roundabout slowly began to turn. Jess and Wayne tore up the embankment and then collapsed, panting.

The flames came almost at once, bursting from the hall in a gush of searing red. Smoke billowed from the windows and they could hear a terrible roaring. The upper storey of Holloway House was bright with light and the swing swung harder and the roundabout turned faster. Doors slammed everywhere and the weather vane on the roof began to turn crazily. They gazed at it in awe, but then Jess seemed to see something else. Horrified, he realized that the faces of terrified children were pressed to the window. He was sure he could make out Caspar, waving and choking and crying for help as the smoke billowed around him.

Jess stood up and Wayne tried to pull him down.

"He's just a kind of echo. Just something left behind. He died on the track. You saw him."

"He's frightened of fire," said Jess. "There's still *something* of him in there. Something. And it's frightened."

"There's nothing," insisted Wayne.

But Jess tore himself away and began to run back down the embankment and up through the grounds. He ran under the crazily moving swing to the door at the end of the corridor from which smoke was now pouring. Jess looked up at the window and again saw Caspar's face. He looked desperate.

"Help me, Jess," he shouted.

Somehow, Jess managed to penetrate the smoke-filled corridor. He could dimly hear the sirens of the fire brigade as he staggered into the blue dormitory. At first he could see nothing there, then he could just pick out a dim outline. It was a bed and there was a child on it.

"Help me, Jess." The words were the most fragile whisper.

"Where's Frank?"

"Frank is always here," said Caspar. "Help me."

"Come to me." Jess's voice was firm.

The figure on the bed seemed to leap at him and he felt something soft and insubstantial in his arms.

"You're dead," whispered Jess.

"I'm waiting. I'm always waiting here."

"There won't be anywhere to wait soon."

"The ground," the little figure muttered. "The earth."

"The fire will destroy that."

Jess choked as smoke poured up into the dormitory. Suddenly he could see a small figure standing in the doorway.

"It's only a firework," said Frank. His voice was soft and gentle. "Come on, Cas. This way. No one's going to hurt you."

The smoke seemed to thin as he spoke and, still clutching something that was more like smoke itself, Jess ran down the circular staircase. At the door stood Frank. But this time he was a man.

"Come on," he said. "This way out. Wayne's here."

Jess looked down at his arms. He was still carrying something – just a wisp – as he ran out of the door.

"I love you, Jess," came the whisper and Jess looked back at the house.

The flames were flickering and Frank the boy was standing looking down from the blue dormitory. He waved.

HAUNTINGS by Hippo Books is a new series of excellent ghost stories for older readers.

Ghost Abbey by Robert Westall
When Maggie and her family move into a run-down old abbey, they begin to notice some very strange things going on in the rambling old building. Is there any truth in the rumour that the abbey is haunted?

Don't Go Near the Water by Carolyn Sloan
Brendan knew instinctively that he shouldn't go near Blackwater Lake. Especially that summer, when the water level was so low. But what was the dark secret that lurked in the depths of the lake?

Voices by Joan Aiken
Julia had been told by people in the village that Harkin House was haunted. And ever since moving in to the house for the summer, she'd been troubled by violent dreams. What had happened in the old house's turbulent past?

The Nightmare Man by Tessa Krailing
Alex first sees the man of his darkest dreams at Stackfield Pond. And soon afterwards he and his family move in to the old house near the pond — End House — and the nightmare man becomes more than just a dream.

A Wish at the Baby's Grave by Angela Bull
Desperate for some money, Cathy makes a wish for some at the baby's grave in the local cemetery. Straight afterwards, she finds a job at an old bakery. But there's something very strange about the bakery and the two Germans who work there. . .

The Bone-Dog by Susan Price
Susan can hardly believe her eyes when her uncle Bryan makes her a pet out of an old fox-fur, a bone and some drops of blood — and then brings it to life. It's wonderful to have a pet which follows her every command — until the bone-dog starts to obey even her unconscious thoughts. . .

All on a Winter's Day by Lisa Taylor
Lucy and Hugh wake up suddenly one wintry morning to find everything's changed — their mother's disappeared, the house is different, and there are two ghostly children and their evil-looking aunt in the house. What has happened?

The Old Man on a Horse by Robert Westall
Tobias couldn't understand what was happening. His parents and little sister had gone to Stonehenge with the hippies, and his father was arrested. Then his mother disappeared. But while sheltering with his sister in a barn, he finds a statue of an old man on a horse, and Tobias and Greta find themselves transported to the time of the Civil War. . .

Look out for these forthcoming titles in the HAUNTING series:
The Rain Ghost by Garry Kilworth
The Haunting of Sophy Bartholomew by Elizabeth Lindsay

HIPPO CLASSICS

HIPPO CLASSICS is a series of some of the best-loved books for children.

Black Beauty by Anna Sewell £1.50
Black Beauty is a magnificent horse: sweet-tempered, strong and courageous, coloured bright black with one white foot and a white star on his forehead. His adventures during his long and exciting life make one of the most-loved animal stories ever written.

Alice's Adventures in Wonderland
by Lewis Carroll £1.50
When Alice sees the White Rabbit scurry by, her curiosity gets the better of her and she follows him down a rabbit hole. Suddenly she finds herself in an extraordinary world of mad tea parties, grinning Cheshire cats, lobster quadrilles and many more wonderful scenes and characters.

Wind in the Willows by Kenneth Grahame £1.50
One spring day Mole burrows out of the ground and makes his way to the river. There he meets Water Rat and is introduced to all Ratty's friends – Badger, Otter and the loveable and conceited Toad. There's an adventure-filled year ahead for all the animals in this classic story.

Kidnapped by R L Stevenson £1.50
David Balfour is cheated of his rightful estate and then brutally kidnapped. He manages to escape – but is forced to go on the run again when he's wrongfully accused of murder. An action-packed tale of treachery and danger.

The Railway Children by E Nesbit £1.50
The lives of Roberta, Peter and Phyllis are changed completely after the dreadful evening when their father is taken away. They move to the country, where they miss their friends and parties and trips to the zoo. Then they discover the nearby railway, and soon the children find their days filled with adventure.

Heidi by Johanna Spyri £1.50

An orphan, Heidi is left with her old grandfather who lives high in the mountains. Heidi soon learns to love her life with the kindly old man, the mountains, the goats, Peter the goat boy, and the people of the village. Then one day she is taken away to Frankfurt, and has to leave her friends far behind . . .

The Hound of the Baskervilles
by Arthur Conan Doyle £1.50

The Baskerville Curse has laid its deadly finger on every member of the family for hundreds of years. When the new heir, Sir Henry, arrives from Canada to claim his inheritance, he asks Sherlock Holmes for his help against the dreadful curse. And with his good friend Dr Watson, Holmes becomes embroiled in one of the most thrilling investigations of his career.

Look out for these titles in the HIPPO CLASSICS series:
A Christmas Carol by Charles Dickens £1.50
Little Women by Louisa M Alcott £1.50
White Fang by Jack London £1.50
Treasure Island by R L Stevenson £1.50

You'll find all these, and many more Hippo books, at your local bookseller, or you can order them direct. Just send off to *Customer Services, Hippo Books, Westfield Road, Southam, Leamington Spa, Warwickshire CV33 0JH*, not forgetting to enclose a cheque or postal order for the price of the book(s) plus 30p per book for postage and packing.